MW01538820

REDACTED

CONFESSIONS OF A CONSPIRACY SMITH

A NOVEL BY
CHAD ALLAN JONES

© 2021 Chad Jones. All rights reserved. No part of this publication may be reproduced, distributed, or transmitted in any form or by any means, including photocopying, recording, or other electronic or mechanical methods, without the prior written permission of the publisher, except in the case of brief quotations embodied in critical reviews and certain other noncommercial uses permitted by copyright law. For permission requests, contact info@redactedbook.com.

This is a work of fiction. Any resemblance to actual events or persons, living or dead, is entirely coincidental.

For Carrie…

PROLOGUE

THE CON OF TRUTH

Margo Cavanaugh had decided that everything about the so-called VerityCon was a lie. It claimed to be about seeking untold truths about the universe, but like all cons, it was only ever about money. The convention was in two ballrooms of a run-down hotel on the outskirts of Sedona. The windows of the hotel were filled pane-to-pane with poorly-drawn tempera-paint murals of gray aliens and flying saucers. The hotel bar had been wrapped in green Christmas lights and its chalkboard menu had been littered with pun-based drinks and sandwiches. She'd tried the 'Marstini' and the 'Flying Saucer Swiss Burger' the night before and had been unimpressed. They were watered down and overcooked, respectively.

The hotel itself had seen better days. It might have been charming when it had been built, but the seventies' aesthetic of the Calloway Hotel combined with the worn, bizarrely-patterned carpets and peeling paint just made it seem old and tired. The air had a stale musk, making Cavanaugh wonder how many days, weeks, or months her room had gone unoccupied before she dropped off her suitcase and made a bee-line for the cheapest whiskey she could find.

She looked out to the small crowd of the convention hall. And what would normally be filled with crowds of Arizonans eager to listen to a get-rich-quick real estate seminar, meditating their way to their better selves, or attending what she could only imagine the cheapest wedding reception in modern history, was wall-to-wall with uncomfortable folding chairs. Filling less than a quarter of them were those seeking answers.

Cavanaugh had spent little time moving though the booths of the convention floor in the adjacent ballroom. She'd passed the t-shirts, crystals, artists, and cosplayers on her way to Authors' Row. She walked past stacks of self-published books on Roswell, ancient technologies, the real history of Sumeria, proof of alien DNA in the human genome, past lives, and the hidden meanings of the Egyptian Pyramids. She spent five dollars on a book entitled *The Carolina Project: What We Know They're Not Telling Us About Kitty Hawk: The Definitive Truth* out of morbid curiosity about what the author might think they know about it. She had to bow out of the conversation when the author, a skeletally-thin man with a shaggy, unkempt beard and wild, sunken eyes, went into rambling detail about his research. If the author's conversational skills were any indication, she was not expecting the prose to be anything but more of the same.

She dragged her rolling suitcase, wandering the floor until she came to her own, sad little plastic table covered in a white sheet. She unfolded her vinyl banner with her name in bold letters and spread out her wares quickly. At least, she had thought, her books weren't photocopied and spiral bound at the local print shop as some of them had been. *The Saturn Bell* had won a few awards. *Jupiter's Eye* had done well enough to get the attention of Hollywood, and a producer who did not really understand it. Copies of her new book, *Confessions of a Conspiracy Smith*, fresh from the printer, took up the most room on her table. The still-drying ink stung her nose when she opened her suitcase.

There, she had sat for the better part of the morning. In that time, she sold two copies of *The Saturn Bell*. Later, she autographed a well-worn paperback of *Jupiter's Eye* with 'To my No. One Fan,' punctuated with her doctor's scrawl of a signature. She sold only one copy of *Conspiracy Smith*, and had several passersby take a promotional postcard from her table without bothering to make eye contact. A few would-be writers asked for advice. The erratic stream of people ebbed and flowed as the morning passed.

She could not shake the feeling of being watched. She could not help but scan the crowd for familiar faces.

There was a steady hum of conversation, and indistinguishable chatter from a nearby lecturer. Larger panels were held in the adjacent ballroom. Smaller panels, like her own reading scheduled for later that morning, were separated from the main convention hall with curtains. This turned whatever topic was being discussed into a dull roar. The loudest noise on the floor came from a heavy-set man standing on a box to elevate himself above the heads and shoulders of the crowd, practically screaming that their used books were half-price.

She cracked the cap of a bottled water, and waited for her hangover to go away. It didn't. The dull ache kept her company until the alarm on her phone let her know that it was time to go. She had two things on her calendar. The reading now, and 'The Big Show' panel discussion later this afternoon. The truth, as it should be at VerityCon, was she looked forward to neither.

She quickly locked her books into a rolling suitcase, and set out a card that read, 'Back Soon.' This was, she guessed, probably a lie. Whether or not she would even bother coming back after the reading or if she'd just head straight to the bar was still to be determined.

She checked her phone and swore. By the time she finished packing, she was already a few minutes late. She shouldered her satchel and made her way through the crowd to Room Four. A volunteer in a black tee with the Con's ubiquitous logo on it raised her head from her clipboard and saw Cavanaugh coming.

"Margo Cavanaugh?" The young woman's face went from worried-annoyed to just worried.

Cavanaugh nodded, "Morning. Where do you want me?"

"Through there, five minutes ago." The woman sighed

and pointed to a small alleyway of curtains between the two speaking areas.

Cavanaugh considered snapping at her, but thought better of it. All she could manage was a sheepish, "Sorry." She followed the volunteer towards the back wall and then ducked inside the curtain. As she made her way, she could hear her neighbor's lecture was already passed welcoming the crowd and deep into his presentation about how Egyptians had used electric lightbulbs to light their way as they built the pyramids.

The volunteer stopped at a laptop sitting on a folding chair with video cables running behind the back curtain. She pressed a button on the keypad and turned to Cavanaugh and showed the slide on the screen.

"That good?" she asked. "We added the black on the sides, because the aspect ratio we got was all wrong."

"Must be some kind of grand conspiracy," Cavanaugh muttered. She hadn't examined the slide closely. A precursory glance told her it was the key art image she had sent, if a little stretched thanks to the aforementioned incorrect ratio. "Good enough."

She peeked through the curtain to the neatly-arranged white folding chairs zip-tied together into neat rows. Her heart sank when she saw that there was only a half-dozen people scattered in a space that could hold a hundred and fifty.

The volunteer turned and held up a hand to Cavanaugh. "I'll be here for a few minutes to make sure everything's working. Then, I got to run and you're on your own. Cool?"

"Cool," Cavanaugh said as she dug through her satchel. "Ready?"

Cavanaugh pulled out a copy of her book, decorated with sticky-notes sticking out from its pages, and a metal water bottle. She took a quick swig and then nodded to the volunteer. The warmth of the whiskey inside the bottle spread through her throat.

"Am now. Let's do it."

The volunteer raised her eyebrow, curious about what was actually in the bottle. Cavanaugh assumed she could smell what was inside.

"Is there a problem?" Cavanaugh asked.

The volunteer shrugged and slipped between a seam in the curtain and took to the wooden stage and adjusted the microphone with a squeal. The volunteer never took her eyes off of her clipboard as she read, "Morning everybody! We are very pleased to present the award-winning author of *The Saturn Bell*, Margo Cavanaugh with a reading from her latest book, *Confessions of a Conspiracy Smith*. Put your hands together, please!"

A few did. The others had their noses down in their convention booklets. A sad realization hit her that they might not even be here for her, but were camped out for whatever was next in the space. Cavanaugh stepped out, and saw that not even her Number One Fan was here.

She made her way to the podium and took a deep breath. Behind her, washed out by the light of the projector, was her name, and the title of her book, and a photo. She was now ten years older than she was in that headshot, and she glanced back at that posed, black and white lie with a perfect head-tilt. Her hair was now shorter, and a shock of blue accented her natural gray. Her wide, silver cat-eye glasses hid the spreading crow's feet and bloodshot eyes.

The woman she had been in the photo hadn't yet gone through hell, but she would. Margo Cavanaugh was no longer that woman, and she knew it.

Her nerves were as calm as the shot of whiskey allowed. The hangover had subsided, but there was still a dull thud coming from the back of her mind. A few — she was hesitant to call them fans — were scattered among the uncomfortable chairs arranged in neat rows.

She leaned into the microphone with a tiny squeal of feedback. "I'd like to thank everyone for coming. Before we begin, I'd like to start with a story."

"When I was six years old," she said, "I was riding my bike near my grandfather's farm. It was just after dusk and I was with my uncle, who was just a few years older than me." As she spoke, she remembered the creak of the wheel, and the smell of the mud after a fresh rain.

"We took a dirt road that followed a creek bed when I saw it. An alien. Large, gray-skinned, almond-eyed, and wearing a hooded robe."

She remembered the shock, and the palpable terror that she felt. She remembered the scream she made. The few that were in the crowd straightened in their seats. They turned to each other and leaned in, listening intently.

"This thing stepped from behind a tree, and reached for me. I screamed, I ran, and when we got back to the farmhouse, everyone had a great laugh. Another of my uncles had been waiting for us in an old Halloween costume."

She remembered the embarrassment she felt, and the bellowing laughter of her grandmother.

And the fundamental betrayal.

"Since then, I've always approached anything, and I mean anything — religion, aliens, ghosts, psychics, news, anything presented as a *fact* — with skepticism. And I can say from experience, don't believe everything you're told. We, as humans, are wired for storytelling. We are *all* storytellers."

She paused to take another swig from her water bottle. Cavanaugh opened the copy of her book.

"And all storytellers are liars."

CHAPTER ONE

LET'S TALK ABOUT ALIENS

— 1.1 —

The second Mad Autumn stepped onto the stage, every person in the ballroom broke into rapt applause. She broadly feigned surprise at the reaction and made her way to the podium with a burlesque strut. There was, by her guesstimate, a zero-point-zero-percent chance of not getting laid tonight if that was what she wanted. She loved having fans, and by the whoops in the audience, they were out there in force. She waved to the them, and greeted the crowd with a broad, come-hither smile. Mad Autumn wore black, thick-rimmed Buddy Hollys and a black sports jacket over a tie-dye t-shirt that read 'The Truth is Far Out There.' And if anyone were to ask her, she was rocking it.

"Well, hello there, VerityCon," she called, and the response was an enthusiastic roar from the crowd. She broke into a wide smile, and added with a cartoonishly-breathy voice, "You're all looking particularly sexy tonight."

She added a perfectly-executed James Brown spin, and flipped her green-streaked hair. She adjusted her glasses and leaned into the mic.

"Can I get an, 'ello aliens!'?" she added with an objectively terrible British accent. And, on cue, they responded. Mad Autumn knew her audience. She winked to a group in the front row.

"I'm so, so glad to see so many believers out there," she said, sparking the crowd to clap in response. "This is 'Aliens Through The Ages.' I am your moderator, Mad Autumn Madigan from the *Zings from Another World* podcast. I know a thing or two about the paranormal, the para-terrestrial, and the para-spiritual, and so does our esteemed panel. So, let's meet them, shall we? From the hit show *Alien Truth*, author, anthropologist, ufology expert, and my personal hero, give it up for the one, the only, the incredibly, incredibly sexy Dr. Gerry Henry."

A man with a wild shock of white hair and circular glasses burst on the stage to wild applause from the moderate crowd. Henry raised his arms like a rock star and the crowd cheered harder. Mad Autumn clapped, and gave a low, exaggerated bow to the man. They kissed each other's cheek, and Henry took his seat at the table behind a small placard with his name on it. He grabbed the bottled water in front of him, and immediately cracked it open.

"Am I that sexy?" he asked into the microphone in front of him.

"Absolutely, baby," Mad Autumn cooed, and this drew a long 'woo' from the crowd. She winked at him, and knew that her earlier assessment of her potential sexual conquests would be one-hundred percent accurate.

She flipped to her next note card. "Ladies, gentlemen, and aliens hiding among us disguised as ladies and gentlemen, I give you magician, medium, fellow podcaster, and the creator-editor-in-chief-slash-publisher of *The Unknown Journal*, Professor Abraham Stanislav."

Henry raised his bottled water in salute and shouted with glee. "Get out here, Abe!"

A rail-thin man dressed in a striped, purple suit took the stage by throwing the curtains aside and eyeing the crowd. His hair was slicked back, and his pencil-thin mustache and comically-bushy eyebrows made him seem like something from another age — as if he stepped, fully-formed, from a Victorian Era circus poster. Abe Stanislav shook Mad Autumn's hand and gave it a gentle kiss before taking his seat next to Henry.

"I knew you were going to say that, Gerry." The mic in front of him echoed his words through the ballroom. The audience burst into a chuckle.

Gerry slapped him on the shoulder with glee. "Good to see you, buddy."

Mad Autumn eyed the men on the stage. "You guys are dead sexy, you know that?" She turned to the crowd. "Aren't they?" The crowd again, cheered at her command, and she loved it.

She flipped to the next card. "So, I hate to say this, but our third panelist, Dr. Hamilton Boley from the Tomorrow Institute was not able to make it today. I know, hold your 'boos,' please. Doctor Tomorrow sends his regrets. But," she paused, soaking in the moment. "But, we have someone who was kind enough to step in, last minute. So, for our final panelist for 'Aliens Through the Ages,' please welcome to the stage, the author of such sci-fi thrillers as *The Saturn Bell*, *Jupiter's Eye*, and her brand new thriller that I cannot wait to read, *Confessions of a Conspiracy Smith*, Margo Cavanaugh."

Mad Autumn held her breath, unsure how the audience would actually react. Doctor Tomorrow had written six books connecting the history of the Sumerian Annunaki sky gods to a secret society. He'd been a repeated guest on both Henry's *Alien Truth* and Stanislav's podcast. Cavanaugh, on the one hand, wrote a book that some of these people might have heard of. When Cavanaugh stepped onto the stage, she looked tired to Mad Autumn. No, not tired. Mad Autumn thought she looked hung over.

Cavanaugh edged cautiously onto the stage, and the applause dulled from the roars for Henry and Stanislav to a polite clap. 'Bookish and trying too hard' was Mad Autumn's assessment. Her spiky gray hair had a streak of bright blue and was complemented by her silver glasses.

Cavanaugh gave the slightest of waves to the crowd, and moved to her chair with her shoulders slumped. She barely even made eye contact with either Henry or Stanislav. Margo Cavanaugh simply took her seat and reached for the bottled water. Mad Autumn was not at all impressed with her stage presence.

Cavanaugh leaned into her mic, and received a horrific screech of feedback for her efforts. "Thanks for having me," she said.

Mad Autumn saw Cavanaugh scanning the thin crowd as if she were searching for someone. After a moment, the other woman relaxed and turned to Mad Autumn.

"Okay," Cavanaugh said, showing the first signs of life. "So. Let's talk about aliens, shall we?"

— 1.2 —

Ten years ago, along a lone stretch of desert road...

When he realized his car had drifted into the opposite lane, Mitchell Vincent pulled the wheel to straighten his course. He was never in any danger, as he hadn't seen another car for the better part of ten minutes, and, by now it was pushing midnight. Admittedly, he should have had his eyes on the road and not on the sky, but, according to his notebook, it had been almost six weeks — specifically, thirty-nine days — since he'd seen the swirling, triangular lights in the skies above along the highway.

The first time he saw them, he hadn't been prepared. He caught the motion out of the corner of his eye, and didn't think to pull over until they took a hard left, and vanished over the nearby rocky ridge. The turn they had made had to have been less than ninety degrees. At first he'd taken it for a low-flying aircraft, or some kind of drone. But the lights didn't move like an airplane, and whatever it was, it was too big to be a drone. It wasn't until he was at his closest point that he saw that the lights were not just arranged in three rotating sets of three, but the lights themselves appeared to be triangular.

On that night, thirty-nine days ago, Mitchell had taken Highway 44 home after a spectacularly long day at the insurance office. He sometimes took this route, a good twenty minutes out of his way, on days when he had to decompress after a particularly rough day of combing over policies of claims. Usually, he put on some slow, calming music and drove until he felt the stress and frustrations generated by the day's events subside. That had been his routine to alleviate his tension before taking it home to Danielle and Allie.

His doctor had asked him to work on his stress — and, for what it's worth, the doctor had also given him the old song and dance of eating better and exercising — so, before he went home, Mitchell developed the routine to help him maintain his calm. But, since that night, he'd not been able to focus. He'd not been able to do much of anything.

Sleep was near impossible until his mind was so exhausted he couldn't help but drift away. In the early hours of one of those sleepless nights, he'd sketched out what he'd thought he'd seen. He haunted the usual chatrooms to see if anyone else had any information on the triangular lights.

He'd hoped that there was someone out there that might have seen what he'd seen. The closest he came was some rumor of dancing lights above San Bernardino, but nothing like the triangles in the Arizona sky that he had witnessed.

His wife, Danielle, worried about him, and had told him as much. He'd promised Danielle he'd try, but that turned out to be a promise he would not be able to keep.

He'd waited for her to drift off before getting behind the wheel and driving out to the spot along Highway 44. He'd seen the lights at 11:44, (which could not possibly have been a coincidence, he reasoned) and used that information as the basis of a spreadsheet he'd created to keep track of his journeys. At a picked time, he'd drive along the road, hoping to see the lights again. Hoping he'd be able to capture it the next time he saw it. And secretly hoping that it hadn't been some kind of stress-induced hallucination. Or worse yet, him just flat-out losing his mind in the same way his grandmother had done in her final days.

He'd bought a dash cam and upgraded his phone to make sure he had the best camera possible. After every run, he'd pore over the dash cam footage to see if it had caught anything he might have missed while driving. The closest he came was an unexplained flash of light over the ridge along the road, but nothing like what he had seen thirty-nine days ago.

Mitchell adjusted the dash cam and slowed his car to a crawl. By the mile-marker, and his own studying of maps, this was the place. This was the time. And this was the night he'd been waiting for for weeks.

When he saw a series of spinning lights arranged in a triangular formation rising over the ridge, he almost didn't believe his own eyes. He sucked in a breath and held it for a heartbeat. It was not his imagination. It was not a mistake. It was there.

It was real.

Mitchell let out the breath he'd been holding in a sharp burst. His hands trembled as he reached for the dash cam, his eyes darting from the small screen of the camera, and aimed it to the ridge, slightly adjusting the digital zoom.

The lights swirled in the sky.

Mitchell pulled against the seatbelt before remembering to unbuckle it. He threw the car door open and snatched his phone from the holder hooked into the air conditioning vent. He tried to get the phone up and running without taking his eyes off the thing.

"What the hell?" he whispered. "What the hell is it?"

Mitchell shielded his eyes. The lights in the distance spun and whirled, and he could hear an eerie hum, like a mechanical heartbeat in the night sky. He could see something he hadn't seen before. There was a dark shadow cast against the star field of the night sky. The silhouette was formed from two, moving switchblade-like wings jutting from a central, triangular shape.

Mitchell caught his breath, and looked around. He was alone on the road. He soaked in the sight. He had to remind himself that what he was seeing was actually happening.

"It's real," he muttered. "It's real!" Mitchell raised his phone to get the object into frame. He raced to the edge of the road and the electrified fence that made the ridge beyond inaccessible.

Above, the lights spun in the distance, like stars gone mad. As it moved back and forth along an irregular pattern, Mitchell did his best to keep his phone steady. The whatever-it-was flying over the ridge wobbled, as if struggling to stay in the air. Its movements were erratic, hovering as if it were drunk, and Mitchell was having difficulty anticipating the object's flight.

"It's February fourth," he began, his voice shaking with excitement. "Approximately 11:45 p.m. I don't know what I'm seeing. There are these six triangular lights — I hope I'm getting this — six lights, spinning in a counter-clockwise pattern. It appears to be some kind of craft. I've never seen anything like it. There's this hum, I guess? Like a heartbeat. Not sure if it's loud enough for the camera to pick that up. This is the second time I've witnessed this phenomenon, and I have absolutely no idea what it is."

Mitchell watched as the craft steadied itself. Once the triangular shape leveled, it darted around the sky at breakneck speeds and then dove behind the ridge. Gone in an instant. A moment later the last of the light and the low, mechanical noise faded until the only sound Mitchell could hear was the thundering of his own heart.

"It's gone back over the ridge, whatever it was." Mitchell said, still recording. He then turned the camera back to himself. He wiped his mouth and exhaled. "It's real," he whispered, as a tear slid out of the corner of his eye.

"God, it's real."

— 1.3 —

Danielle Vincent sat at her dining room table, feeling the coffee mug in her hands slowly cool over the last hour. She tried to watch television, tried reading, tried to distract herself by aimlessly scrolling online, but nothing had worked. She'd checked on Allie four times in the last two hours only to find her daughter deep in sleep.

Danielle hadn't been able to get back to sleep since she rolled over to find that Mitchell was not in bed. Not in the house. And with his car missing in the driveway. The shock of adrenaline in her system had slowly given way to the old panic creeping up her spine. They were supposed to be past this. He'd been acting manic. His moods were swinging more and more wildly over the last month. He'd been increasingly both manic and melancholy. And this was not the first time she'd woken up to find him not in bed, with the car missing.

He'd always come back in the middle of the night and crawl into bed trying to be as quiet as possible. She'd always just lain there, pretending to sleep. And when she was certain that he had drifted off, she would watch him.

Danielle had come to two possible conclusions. Either he was having an affair, or, more likely, had stopped taking his medication. He didn't smell of sex, at least, but there was a quiet sadness to his face. A sadness mixed with a perpetual worry.

Ever since he came home a few weeks ago, claiming to see something along the highway, he'd been acting increasingly anxious. He'd become withdrawn, but she could tell something was festering in his thoughts. On those nights when Mitchell would quietly sneak away and just as quietly sneak back, Danielle cried herself back to sleep.

But, she promised herself, not tonight.

She sat there for another hour, staring into nothingness until the flash of headlights panned the house as Mitchell's car rolled into the driveway. She steeled herself, taking a bitter swig of cold coffee. She wasn't sure which Mitchell was going to step through that door.

The manic, or the melancholy.

Danielle Vincent realized her answer immediately as Mitchell's rapid footsteps raced to the door. She braced herself, and her body was flooded with adrenaline once more as the door swung open with a bang.

"Danielle!" Mitchell burst into the house with his phone in his shaking hands. His face was flushed, and he crossed the living room to reach her. She tensed as he sat at the table.

"Where have you been?" she snapped, trying to keep her voice low. Danielle stared at her husband. She crossed her arms as if to protect herself from the madness overtaking his eyes. There were times when his body would build up tolerances to the chemical cocktail that kept his depression and paranoia in check. She wondered if this was becoming one of those times.

"Danielle," he said, offering the phone to her with both hands. "I saw it! I saw it!"

Danielle remained calm. She tried not to react.

"I, I saw it. I got it." He slapped the phone on the table, and spun it towards her. His fingers fumbled to open it. "On this, and on the dash cam."

Danielle forced herself to uncross her arms. Tried to make herself be calm. "What? You saw what, exactly?"

"Those lights along the ridge. I saw them again."

Danielle held herself back. Not for the first time in her life, she choked down the anger and the worry. She didn't want to shut down. She knew that she had to be calm for both of them. But she knew she couldn't.

Her words came out more exasperated than she intended. "Mitchell? Just — "

Mitchell opened the phone, he scrolled through the files in his library. "I got it on camera this time," he said. "This time I was ready, Danny. This time I have proof!"

Her hands fiddled with her coffee mug. "This has gone way beyond hobby, hon. This is bordering on obsession."

"Don't say anything until you see it."

"Mommy? What's going on?" They turned at the small, worried voice to see their daughter, Allie. The four-year-old stepped from the darkness of the hallway. Her dark hair was like that of her father, but she had her mother's eyes. She wore her cartoon lamb pajamas and carried a stuffed rabbit in the crook of her arm.

Danielle said under her breath to Mitchell, "You're scaring Allie."

Mitchell tensed, but shook it off. He knelt to be on the same level as his daughter, "Don't worry, Bunny-bun. Everything is just fine."

At her nickname, Allie brightened. She craned her head up to her Daddy and beamed. She squeezed her rabbit. "Okay, Daddy."

Mitchell called her over and kissed her head. "Want to see something incredible?"

Allie nodded vigorously, but, Danielle's jaw clenched. Allie hopped up on her father's lap, and he wheeled the phone around to show her. Danielle rose from her seat to get a better view of the phone.

"Mitchell?" Danielle said, hoping Mitchell would take the cue and not drag Allie into this. He didn't appear to take the hint.

"It's fine," he said.

"What is this?" Danielle asked.

Mitchell just raised a finger. "Watch," he said. "Just watch. You'll see. You'll see I'm right."

Danielle watched the video and saw three sets of lights whirling in darkness. But whatever Mitchell thought he was seeing, she only saw blurry dots of light moving through the night sky. She heard his frantic narration from the weak speakers on the phone. The image dipped in and out of focus as the camera tried to adjust for the rapidly moving lights, automatically compensating for his car's headlights. Just as soon as the lights disappeared back over the ridge on the recording, Mitchell turned to her, with an expectant smile on his lips.

Allie turned to her mother, a confused expression on her face. "Mommy?"

Danielle pulled Allie from Mitchell's lap and held her. The girl was getting heavier every day. Danielle kissed her daughter on the head and sat in the chair next to him, and exhaled.

"Honey," she said, "what *is* this? What is this supposed to be?"

Mitchell shook his head, she could see the excitement building in him. But more than that, a nervous anxiety she'd seen before was also building in him.

"I don't know, I don't know," he kept repeating the phrase as he fidgeted with his hands. He caught himself doing it and placed them on the table to stop them.

"I have to tell someone. I have to tell everyone," Mitchell said. He saw her worried expression, and his brow furrowed. "You don't believe me? You just saw it, and you don't — even with this in front of you, you don't believe me." He banged his fist on the table and both Danielle and Allie jumped. He let out a frustrated, guttural moan.

His flash of anger disappeared as quickly as it had appeared.

"What is this supposed to be?" she repeated in as calm of a voice as she could manage.

"Isn't it obvious? It's proof," he said, his words coming out in quick bursts. "Proof of extraterrestrial crafts. Proof that they're working with the government. There's a government facility, a military base or something, past that fence. It has to be connected to that. They have to be either watching us, or working with us. I know it."

"'They' who?" Danielle asked. "Aliens?"

Mitchell nodded as if the answer was obvious. "And now that you've seen it, now, do you believe me? Everyone will want to see this. Everyone *has* to see this. This changes everything."

Mitchell must have sensed her hesitation. She wasn't able to hide the doubt in her mind, and he must have seen it in her eyes as he stiffened. He straightened in his chair and offered her the phone with the video paused on an image of the whirling lights.

"You have to believe me, Danny," Mitchell pleaded. "It's real. I have the dash cam footage, too. It's steadier. I couldn't get as close but it's steadier. I'll get it."

Danielle grabbed his arm and squeezed. "I don't know what to say."

"Say you're seeing what I'm seeing. Say you believe me," he said. "Say you don't think I'm crazy."

Allie tugged on her father's sleeve. "Are they aliens, Daddy?"

Mitchell leaned down to his daughter. "We don't —"

Danielle gave her daughter as reassuring a smile as she could. "It's just a bunch of lights, Allie. It's nothing to worry about, promise."

Mitchell opened his mouth to protest, but Danielle's glare silenced him. She could see his mind racing.

"Allie, hon," Danielle stood. "Let's go back to bed, huh? You don't have to worry about any of this. This is talk for adults, not little bunnies."

"But, why?"

Finally taking Danielle's lead, Mitchell reached out, offering his hand to his daughter. Allie quickly snatched it. "Hop along, Bunny-bun. Listen to Mommy."

Defeated, Allie hopped off of her mother's lap. "Okay, Daddy. Come on, Mr. Rabbity." Allie made her way back to her room, dragging her stuffed rabbit by the ears.

Danielle followed her, and helped the girl into bed with a kiss on the forehead. When she heard the front door close, and the car door open, Danielle's warm expression twisted into concern.

"Everything's going to be fine," she told her daughter.

"Is Daddy mad?" she asked.

Danielle contemplated the meanings of that word and wondered if he were, and if they'd ever see 'normal' again. She wondered if they had ever been normal in the first place.

"Everything's going to be fine," she repeated. A second later, she heard the front door open and close again. She tried not to show Allie her tension. She kissed her on the forehead and added, "Get back to sleep, love."

When she made it back to the dining room, Mitchell had the dash cam in his hands, and he was fiddling with the buttons on the back to get it to play. She closed the door to the hallway.

She held her breath and counted to three. Then, she turned to her husband, deathly serious. She spoke in low tones as not to alarm the girl in her room.

"I need this to stop," she said. "This has gone on long enough."

Mitchell was taken aback. "What has to stop?"

She grabbed his phone from the table. "This, Mitchell. I need you to let this go, please. You've been obsessing about this for weeks."

"Did you not just see that?" he asked. "Can you explain what that was?"

"It's just a bunch of lights, Mitchell," Danielle said. "It could be anything. Maybe it's just a weird helicopter or something."

He just scoffed and offered her the dash cam. "Why can't you see what's right in front of you?"

Danielle crossed her arms, and nodded in the direction of Allie's room. "Why can't you? Allie's worried. Her head is full of aliens and spaceships and monsters because you put them there. Are you blind to that? This is an obsession with you. I don't know what out there — "

"Now you've seen it, too!"

"But you know there's an Air Force base out there, you said it yourself."

Mitchell snapped his fingers. "Exactly. What are they hiding out there?"

"It's probably some kind of new aircraft, and that's just what you're seeing," she put her hand on his arm, and, as it had in the past, the gesture calmed him. "Couldn't it be that simple?"

Then, he pulled his arm away. "Can't be. There's no aircraft made by man that can do that," he said. "Name one."

Danielle slumped into a dining room chair. He didn't

want her help, she knew. He wanted her to see what he did. But she couldn't bring herself to do it. "I don't know," she admitted. "And neither do you. Unless you're suddenly an expert on aircraft now."

Mitchell's expression darkened. "You're making fun of me."

"I didn't mean to," she said. "I'm just tired, that's all."

"No," he said. "You're just tired of me, and I'm tired of you ignoring the truth."

Danielle knew she had to remain calm or he would simply shut down, but it was getting harder and harder with every passing day. His mood swings had been getting wilder.

"I love you, but we've been down this road before," she said.

"You've never believed me," he said.

"I just don't want this to get out of control," she said, "like last time."

"Last time," he said and shrunk in shame. Absently, his hand reached for the small scar on his temple. A thing he did unconsciously when he was thinking. "I know, I got a little manic. I know I can be hard to live with. I'm sorry. It's just how I'm wired. I need you to still love me."

"I do," she assured him. "I always have."

"But, last time," he said, getting excited again. "I didn't have video. I didn't have proof. Now I do!"

"What you have is not proof." Danielle didn't mean for her words to sting, but Mitchell recoiled as if he were physically slapped. "You're not sleeping. You're scaring our daughter. You're scaring *me*. You have to let this go. Please. Please, Mitchell."

"Why is this so far outside the realm of possibility that you can't even entertain the thought that I might be right about this?" he asked.

Danielle stared at him. "Because I can't," she said finally. "Because I have other worries in life."

"This is bigger than you can imagine. The government has known about this for — you're being naive!" he shouted.

"And you're being," she began, then trailed off, tired of arguing. "You have to stop. For the sake of your family, you have to stop. I can't keep having this same fight over and over again. I can't pretend we're okay anymore, Mitchell. You know that, right? We're not. I love you, but this — this obsession — it's hard. Please tell me you'll let it go."

Mitchell turns the dash cam over in his hands. Danielle could see the still image of the lights on his screen. He set the camera on the table, and clicked it off.

"I will," he said with a nod, then met her gaze. "I promise." She knew her husband and she knew he meant it.

Danielle felt the tension of the night wash away. She slid into his arms and held him close. "I love you, Mitch." She pulled out of the hug, and kissed him on the cheek. "But I'm tired. Come to bed."

Mitchell kissed her back.

— 1.4 —

Passing his daughter's room, Mitchell heard the girl stirring, and her quiet voice called out.

"Daddy?"

Mitchell poked his head into the room and saw her, practically hiding under the covers with Mr. Rabbity held tight. She was illuminated only by the dim, yellow glow of the nightlight coming from the corner of the room.

"How're you doing, kiddo?" he asked.

"I can't sleep," she said, just above a whisper. Her large, brown eyes blinked at him. She was rarely one to hesitate when speaking, but she chewed her lip in thought. "Are aliens real, Daddy?"

Mitchell wasn't sure what to say. He was suddenly aware of Danielle hovering in the hallway outside their daughter's room.

"Maybe out there somewhere," he said. "It's a big universe."

"But they're not *here?*" she asked, she pulled the blankets up to her nose as if afraid of the answer. "Are they?"

Mitchell hesitated, then shook his head. As much for his daughter as for his wife, he said, "No, they're not here."

"So, you were wrong?"

Mitchell smiled and patted her leg. "We all make mistakes, Bunny-bun."

Allie started to pull herself out from beneath the protection of her blanket. "They're not going to get us?"

"Don't worry. Everything's going to be okay, okay?"

Allie whispered, "Is Mommy mad?"

"No," he said, but instead of seeing relief in her eyes, his words appeared to have the opposite effect.

"Daddy?" Allie struggled with her words. Her brow was scrunched, as if she were not sure how to ask the next question. "Why are you lying?"

Mitchell froze, staring at his daughter. It took him a moment to figure out how to respond. To stall, he just stroked her hair.

"I'm not lying, and that's the truth," he said. He took her stuffed animal and stared directly to its eyes. "I wouldn't lie to Mr. Rabbity, would I?"

Relief filled the girl's eyes. Allie shook her head and grinned at her father. "Thanks, Daddy."

"Go to sleep, little girl," he said, setting the rabbit back into the bed next to her. "I'm putting Mr. Rabbity in charge. If there's any trouble, he'll handle it, okay?"

She grinned, and rolled over pulling her blanket tight. He backed away, and gave her a wink as he turned to the hallway where he found Danielle next to him.

His wife simply mouthed the words, "Thank you."

She stroked his arm, and led him into the bedroom. But long after she had drifted to sleep, Mitchell's mind thought about life in the universe. The rumors of aliens colluding with the government dating back to the forties. About the exponential advancements in technology over the last century. About the videos of alien sightings that he'd seen on the internet, and about the fact that he might have something to add to the conversation.

In his mind's eye, he ran through what he had seen along the highway. Over and over again.

He thought about this until sunlight began to creep in from the horizon. Today, he knew would be a long day, but tonight, he'd post the video to the internet and see if he could find out something on the forums.

CHAPTER TWO

ENTERING THE MAZE

— 2.1 —

"It's easy to go in the wrong direction when the initial trajectory is so entirely wrong," Cavanaugh said to the convention audience from the dais. "The belief that the Annunaki of ancient Sumeria were somehow alien blood royalty is, if you'll forgive the term, unsubstantiated madness."

To Cavanaugh's surprise, the audience audibly gasped.

Mad Autumn checked her notes, clearly incapable of making eye contact with Cavanaugh because she was rolling her eyes. Mad Autumn mouthed the words, 'Oh, Brother,' drawing a roll of laughter from the crowd.

Gerry Henry asked, "Did you not hear a word of what I was saying?"

"Oh, I heard it," Cavanaugh said. "I'm just not having any of it. You can't call supposition and wild theories facts without evidence. I mean, you can, but you'd be a loon."

At this point, Gerry Henry just shook his head. "Wow," he said. He took off his glasses, and with a theatricality worthy of the stage magician to his left, crossed his arms and shot her a smug, self-satisfied smirk. "Just," he added with a broad emphasis, "wow."

"Wow, indeed," Cavanaugh said. "You want to talk about the alien influence on ancient Sumeria, so, let's talk about the source of this belief. Let's talk about the origins of the Annunaki hypothesis. It's claimed that the word 'Annunaki' means, 'Those who from the heavens came.' So, they're totally aliens, right? They created man as a slave race. They came to earth to mine gold for their atmosphere, or some such nonsense."

"I don't know what you're talking about because you don't know what you're talking about," Henry snapped. "Do the work. Research what you're talking about before you stand in front of a crowd of people and embarrass yourself."

The crowd clapped in approval. Henry threw a wink to a clapping fan in the front row.

Cavanaugh forced herself to remain, and sound, calm. "I have. The literal translation of Annunaki is 'princely seed' meaning they're descendants of Anu, the god king. All of the information that suggests that they're extraterrestrial comes from a single, self-proclaimed expert. A man with no concept of the language, no academic credentials, and 'quoting' passages that serve his narrative without even bothering to cite reference. Probably because he thought no one would be able to check his work. He just made it up.

"But, now we can go online and actually read the translations ourselves, which I *have* done," Cavanaugh continued. "I challenge anyone to find the translations that corroborate any credible alien origin for them. All you have to do to see the truth is to look for it. And to want to see it."

— 2.2 —

Ten years ago, in a quiet office building…

The interior of Director Franklin's office was, to Athena Simms' eyes, a mess. The building itself was unremarkable, a brick Georgetown duplex on the edge of the city. Director Franklin himself greeted her in the lobby and led her through the converted office space. Plain-clothes Operatives were packed in gray cubicle walls as tightly as they could. The Operatives chatted over coffee, but quickly hushed as Franklin and Athena got too close. It was what she didn't see in the work-spaces that caught her eye. There were no family photos. No nicknacks, office toys, or, indeed any hint of a person's personality in them. This was clearly a suit-and-tie organization, and she felt horribly underdressed in her jacket and jeans.

Dodging the agency's Operatives moving through the halls, Franklin pointed out various war rooms, conference rooms, and the singular break room smelling of burned coffee. The conference room door was closed with droning muffled voices coming from inside. As a science-fiction writer and amateur ufologist, the conference rooms had names she recognized, 'Roswell,' 'Hangar Eighteen,' and 'Area Fifty-One.' All were connected with the modern extraterrestrial myth. The war room names were more obtuse to her. 'Blackbird,' 'Monty,' and 'Triangle.'

She should not have been surprised when she caught glimpses of the shoulder holsters under some of their jackets, but she was. She inferred from the previous interviews that this was some kind of intelligence work, but she had never been able to quite discern just what branch of government Franklin and his team actually worked for. She was under the impression that this third interview would be an informal formality. She'd already been through numerous screenings, background checks she wasn't sure she would pass, and several conversations with Director Franklin that were so vague as to be meaningless. However, she had to admit the cloak-and-dagger of it all was very intriguing.

But she was not at all clear on why she was, for lack of a better term, being recruited.

Or for that matter, for what.

At the end of the hallway, Franklin opened a large oak

door, revealing the mess of his office. His black, steel desk was covered in stacks of papers, notebooks, and maps. The cleanest area was around a computer and monitor, held into place with black cables locking it to the desk. Multi-colored sticky-notes littered the edges of the monitor, and there were enough stains and crumbs on the desk itself for Athena to infer that the man ate at his desk quite often.

To one side of the desk, a pair of rolling cork boards with every inch filled with photographs, newspaper clippings, pages printed from websites, with each scrap of information strung together by different colored bits of string making a spiderweb of connections. From a cursory glance, the two different boards were two entirely different subjects. One seemed to be centered around a blurry black and white photograph of a wing-like aircraft. The word 'Operation: Montague' was printed in bold letters above.

This must be 'Monty,' she thought.

The other cork board had clippings and strings radiating out from a photograph of a man with a grim expression. From the angle and the quality, it must have come from a security camera. The man was walking along a street carrying a steel briefcase. The various photos and clippings on both were accented with 'x's or check marks. Was this 'Blackbird?' 'Triangle,' or something else entirely?

On the other side of the desk were a set rolling whiteboards. The first was filled with a grid of both names of people and project names. The names were in various colors — black, green, red, and blue — with some of the boxes on the grid filled in to varying degrees. To indicate progress, perhaps. The other was a series of circled words connected to each other, perhaps the results of a brainstorming session. Behind that, the wall was covered with blackboard paint, with seemingly every square inch of it covered in notes, comments, thoughts, and sketches of flying saucers.

By contrast, the man himself was the epitome of neat. A sharp gray suit, thin black tie held in place by a silver clip, and his reddish, blond hair held in place by a generous amount of gel. His eyes were alert and filled with excitement. His mouth was always on the verge of a smile that he could barely contain. If she had to guess, Franklin was a few years younger than she, in his early-to-mid-thirties.

If Franklin's office was nothing short of a one-man war room, he was conducting many wars simultaneously. Everything was, to her surprise, refreshingly analog. Not for the first time that day, Athena wondered just what exactly she had gotten herself into.

"I hope you're ready," he said.

"For what?"

Franklin pulled a stack of books out of a chair and offered for her to sit. The smile that was threatening to escape his lips finally broke and, she had to admit, it was infectious.

"Have you ever heard of 'Majestic?'" he asked, sitting on the edge of his desk for only a moment before getting back up again.

Athena had. She had come across the term researching for her first novel, *The Age of Silver.* "Government misinformation about UFOs from the sixties, right?" she said. "Men in black. Government cover up? Nonsense by all accounts."

"All bunk, indeed." This drew a chuckle from Franklin. Franklin, she noticed, liked to pace behind his desk. She thought back to their previous interactions leading up to this day and wondered if she had ever actually seen him still.

He opened his arms wide. "This is 'Augustus,' the *real* program," he said. "We have offices all over the world. Contacts with major military contractors. Connections with media outlets. This is all highly, highly classified, by the way. Like, treason-level classified if you divulge. You understand this, yes?"

Athena nodded. "I see. Before we go any further, I do have a question. What if I say no to this job? That's what this is? This is a job, right? You've brought me here to offer me a job? Formally? Where I get paid for something?"

Franklin's expression darkened, and Athena felt her blood run cold. "This far in, oh, saying 'no' is not even an option." Then with a wink, his smile returned. "Kidding, of course. I'm not going to lie. I love your work. You were amazing in the think tank exercise. You have a dark and complex mind. One I wish to exploit. Once I saw what you'd come up with, I knew I had to have you."

She squirmed in her chair. Athena's literary agent had gotten her the gig, sitting in a room with a wide variety of writers, engineers, and doctors trying to think of ways terrorists might attack and other doomsday scenarios. It had been a surreal way to get a paycheck, but that was where she first met Franklin.

"Thank you, but I'm not even sure what branch of intelligence you work for."

Franklin tried to physically wave her worry away. "I see you worrying about it; don't worry about it."

She must have tensed, because Franklin quickly added, "Relax, you're going to *love* it. It's unique, and, it's weird. So, listen and listen close. This is as close to an orientation as you're going to get. There are no rules for what we do. There are no company guidelines on this. On any of it.

"Augustus started in the late nineteen-forties with Truman wanting to scare the Russians into thinking we had advanced technology. Flying saucers were all the rage, so, they cooked up the Roswell incident." Franklin held out his hand, as if in apology. "Bonkers idea, I know, but, it was inexpensive and got a lot of press, so they ran with it. But, instead of calling us out on it, the KGB decided they had to counter. We had Roswell. They had Hill 611. We had Area 51. They had Kapsustin Yar."

Athena studied the cork boards and notes on the wall — the chaotic storm of bits of information that surrounded her. Then it hit her. "An arms race of lies."

"Yes! Exactly!" Franklin snapped his fingers, excited. "And neither side dared to blink, so, the lies begat lies, begat alien autopsies, faking faking the moon landing."

"Wait, the moon landing was actually faked?" Athena eyed the man suspiciously. "You can't be serious, there's no way a secret like that could be kept. A conspiracy that large would eat itself."

"No, no, no," he corrected. "We went to the moon. This agency faked that it was faked. We started that narrative. I can neither confirm nor deny that we even paid Kubrick an insane amount of money to drop elements into his work so we could point to it and say, 'Ah, the moon landing was fake and Kubrick did it!' I can neither confirm nor deny that the kid wearing an Apollo sweater in *The Shining* was our doing. That would also be very classified, by the way."

"One would assume," she said.

"But, but, but," Franklin continued, "it's not just the Russians anymore. Certain Iranian circles consider alien influence as an affront against Islam, and an excuse to hate us more. The Chinese have their own agency to control information regarding alien and unusual phenomena. And the North Koreans have started viewing modern tech and history through an extraterrestrial lens."

"But surely they know that it's not, well, real. It's not true, is it?" Franklin laughed again, but she had to ask. "Then why are we doing it?"

"You hit the nail on the head," he said. "It's an arms race of lies. More importantly, the more time and resources foreign powers spend tracking this information, debunking it or making their own, the less they can spend on actual intelligence efforts. We're a shiny object. Another pawn in the intelligence game. Misinformation is relatively cheap to make. A doctored video here. A meme there. But we're kind of a wild card. We're essentially an R&D think tank for intelligence work, especially in the modern era. The stakes are relatively low, so we have the opportunity to experiment. To play. Hell, our work in alien paranoia and promoting the extraterrestrial narrative is essentially the reason we now have a brand new branch of the military, to defend us against us moon people or something. Our department is expanding. We need someone like you."

"Like me?" Athena wasn't sure how to respond other than, "I'm flattered?"

"You should be. This isn't typical intelligence work. It takes a certain venn diagram of skills. Books, games, theater. A multi-disciplined storyteller, like yourself. Now, take a man who sees something he can't explain or understand. Put yourself in his shoes. Like, imagine the first man to see a prototype stealth bomber. What would that have looked like?"

She shrugged. "Like no other plane in the sky."

"Exactly. It would have looked like a damned alien spacecraft. It was revolutionary. How much misdirection did we create by allowing the rumors of alien tech to flourish?" Franklin offered her a piece of paper. "Take a look at this."

Athena examined it, a grainy black and white photo of a dark wedge in the sky with three sets of triangular lights. Not much could be made out from the photo, but it might have been taken in the desert. Arizona, perhaps.

"We have a similar situation," Franklin said. "This is from a video taken by a man named Mitchell Vincent."

She would come to learn this was taken from his car dash cam, and enhanced through photo manipulation. "And that's what he thought he saw? A UFO?"

Franklin resumed his pacing. "He's not the only one. The video is getting some traction online and we need to control that narrative. Get ahead of it as fast as we can.

Make sure they steer as far away from the truth as possible and that anyone who sees this footage thinks it's either a hoax or something extra normal."

"That being?" Athena asked. "What did he really see?"

"Classified," Franklin said. "But suffice it to say, there's rumored to be an airfield on the other side of that fence along the road."

"Why doesn't he believe what he saw was just some kind experimental aircraft?"

This drew a laugh from the man. "We've certainly tried the truth in the past, it simply doesn't always work. Take the whole alien conspiracy movement. Alien visitors among primitive man. Secret extraterrestrial influence in our government."

"Why?" she asked, and she saw Franklin's eyes flash.

"Why do you think that is?" he asked back.

Athena paused, realizing it was a test. She took a breath. "I guess, some are just crazy. Some might just see the world around them and just can't process it. Maybe traditional religions and philosophies don't work, but they're so desperate for answers they'll believe in anything."

"We have an entire contingent of the people who would rather believe that the missing link is alien DNA than try and comprehend the vastness that is the concept of evolution," Franklin said. "They'd rather believe that aliens built the pyramids than that it was done by the tools of the day. And they'd rather believe that their government is hiding aliens than working on experimental aircraft, because for some reason, it's easier for some to accept the concept of otherworldly knowledge than acknowledge the capacity for human genius. And, ultimately, because that's what they want to believe."

Athena shrugged, "The universe can be a hard thing to wrap your head around."

"True," Franklin nodded. "And it doesn't matter what we tell them, what evidence we present, they're going to believe what they want to believe. The more we deny it, the more they believe it."

"You give them questions and let them make their own answers."

"I love it!" Franklin clapped his hands. "You're a natural! I knew it!"

"But, you're preying on their faith."

"Because it works." His eyes darted over his cluttered desk and he picked up a blue file folder. "And now, so do you."

She stared at the offered folder. It was thin, it couldn't have had more than a dozen papers in it. She had to admit, she was intrigued, even if she didn't fully understand what Franklin was asking of her.

"I haven't accepted the position yet," she said. "If you are, in fact, offering me one."

"You will." Franklin shook the folder, tempting. Then, for the first time, Franklin's smile wavered into something more serious. "Your sales have tanked. Your book deal got dropped. The option for *The Age of Silver* fell through. You're broke."

Athena tensed. She'd only heard about *The Age of Silver* a few hours ago from her agent. "How do you — ?"

"We know," he said, leaning back on the edge of this desk. He took a long drink of his coffee. "Here's the thing. Cards on the table, we need you. There aren't many who can do this work, and I believe you might be one of them. We want you because you have a very interesting resume. A playwright, a brilliant if under-appreciated novelist with published hard, sci-fi thrillers, a background in advertising able to write in multiple voices, someone who's made puzzles for computer games. And, frankly, a woman who has nowhere else to go."

Athena felt her heart sink in her chest. *They knew.* Panic raced through her. She tried to remain calm. She had to force herself to breathe.

Almost as if he could read her thoughts, he said, "Don't worry. We know, and we're willing to give you this chance anyway. And if there's anyone who needs a second chance and needs a break, it's you. The question is, are you going to take it?"

Athena hands shook as she took the file folder. Athena rifled through the pages More stills from Mitchell's footage. Online chat transcripts with streaks of yellow and pink highlights marking key points of discussion. A psych profile of Mitchell. A map of the road where he saw the lights. She opened it to see a photo of a man's face, stacked on page after page of typed reports. She stared into his sad eyes. Her finger traced the scar along his brow.

"This Vincent?" she asked. "What do we know about him?"

"Mitchell Vincent, insurance salesman, believer in things extraterrestrial. He thinks he has video of alien aircraft. He doesn't. We want him to continue to believe he does, and convince others of this 'fact.' Married, one child, borderline obsessive-compulsive and manic-depressive. He believes he was abducted by aliens as a child and he's never gotten over it. He's desperate to find proof of his childhood experience; he just hasn't found it yet. That scar on his temple, he thinks it's evidence of his abduction, but records show it's from a car crash he survived as a child."

"Early childhood trauma," Athena observed.

"One that he hasn't been able to shake," Franklin said. "He's very active on the forums. He's the reason we need more people like you. He's a critical thinker; practically a skeptic among those who believe. He's smart, so we have to be smarter. Right now, he thinks he's seen something connected to an alien craft. And we would very much like him to continue believing that."

"We convince him — convince the *skeptic* among the believers — and others will follow." She closed the folder and set it on her lap.

"I love that you get this," he said. "You're going to find out what he knows, then fill in the rest."

Athena shot the man an inquisitive look. "With what, exactly?"

"Ah," he said. "With what, indeed."

Franklin opened his arms and gestured to his cork boards and the complex warren of information that surrounded him. "Entirely up to you. You'll have access to government files for reference and an art department that are foremost experts in forgeries. And —"

Uncertain, Athena fidgeted with the file folder. "You

want me to fake documents, then? What documents?"

"Don't think of it like…" Franklin trailed off and took a sip of his coffee. He pondered what to say next. "If it helps, you're building a narrative around the event. You're a storyteller. So, tell a story. Fake documents. Redact those documents. Leak those documents with hints as to what's been redacted. Everything you make will serve that narrative. To send him in the wrong direction."

Athena eyed the file folder. A smirk tugged at her lips. The earlier panic being replaced by possibilities. For the first time, her gears started turning. What could she do with this? For that matter, *could* she do this? "Laying out pieces to a puzzle that doesn't exist yet. Interesting."

"It absolutely is," he said. "I have a nose for talent, and I have a feeling you'll be great."

"And if I'm not?"

"Well," he said, "let's not find out, shall we? One last piece of advice. Be fluid. Leave gaps for him to fill in. Hint that he's right and let him take it from there. Believe me, people can be wildly imaginative. Adapt the narrative as it unfolds. You're going to be great."

Athena shrugged. "Great at lying? I don't know if I should be flattered."

"You should be. Come on. Don't tell me you weren't born to do this," he goaded. "You wouldn't even be in this office if I didn't think you were the right person for the job. This job. This weird, wonderful, unique opportunity. I hate this idiom, but you have to think outside the box, because there isn't one."

He punctuated his words, tapping the case file. Athena

opened the folder and contemplated for a moment, processing the task.

She pulled out a photo of Mitchell Vincent and stared into his lost, vacant eyes and then to the scar on his temple he considered his proof.

"We're making this up as we go," Franklin admitted. "There's no template for how to do this."

Athena realized what he was saying. "Because, there can't be. If there was a pattern, it'd be noticed." She closed the folder and nodded, understanding. The smirk that had been pulling at the corner of her mouth broke into a full-on smile.

"So, I'd be a Federal Agent? A Woman In Black?"

"Independent contractor, for now." Franklin tensed, ever so slightly. "Technically, you'd be a consultant. Considering your history, we could never officially hire you as an Agent. Sorry."

Athena's smile faded. "I see."

Franklin's infectious enthusiasm picked back up. "You understand what we're asking of you here, right?"

"You want me to tell a story. With flying saucers." For the first time, Athena felt like Franklin was asking something that was within her wheelhouse. She gave him a mock salute. "I'll do my best."

Franklin offered his hand, and she took it. His grip was surprisingly gentle. "Welcome to the United States Department of Misinformation."

"So," she asked, "how *did* they build the pyramids?"

Franklin gave a dismissive shrug. "Oh, who the hell

knows."

— 2.3 —

Franklin led Athena through a wall of cubicles, further and further back into the offices to a dark corner. She carried a file box labeled 'Vincent,' and tried to keep up with Franklin as he waved to the other Agents and Operatives in the hallways.

"We keep tabs on most major conspiracy forums," he said. "As you can imagine there's a great deal of noise. We own a few dozen dummy accounts, making innocuous comments. Mostly bots, popping into a discussion, saying something neutral, like, 'I've never seen anything like that,' or 'Are you sure about your sources?' And whole slew of responses with typos, all caps, and snark."

"And that works?" Athena asked.

Franklin chuckled. "Oh, you have no idea. Sometimes, it requires a human touch to participate in a discussion, and so we'll dip into the forums and write something a little more custom to the situation. When we need one, we turn it over to a project leader, to use as he — *she* — sees fit."

"Like some kind of digital sleeper agent," she said.

"Excellent," he said. His ever-present smile widened. "With them, we have voices we control that have been in the community; that have a history. Some even have a small cabal of friends. Each account is a few years old, so when we do engage with a project it's not from someone who's never been heard of. It adds another layer of credibility when we leak falsified information through them. We'll give you Gemini-with-two-'i's-underscore-twenty-two. It's been gender neutral, if you want to take a more active role yourself."

Athena paused for moment in thought, and raised an eyebrow. "You know this is weird, right?"

"Every day is weirder than the last, for which I am ever grateful." As they reached a cubicle in the corner, Franklin waved his arm in presentation. "Welcome home, Ms. Simms."

The office was small, with little more than a file cabinet, notebook and pens, chair, and a desktop computer that appeared far from state-of-the-art.

"Remember, it has to appear legitimate. Authenticity is paramount," he said. "The key here is the details. We've been busted once because we used a two-letter state abbreviation in an address on a document dated before that became a thing. Hell, one of our guys referenced the hidden symbolism in the St. Louis Arch in a document dated five years before it was built and the forums nailed us for it. Vincent himself was part of that group."

Athena lowered herself into the chair and swiveled to face Franklin. "Got it. What about Mitchell Vincent? What's his level of activity?"

Franklin reached past her and turned on her computer. "It's spiked considerably since he posted his video. It's starting to get traction on the forums, so we need to act quickly. The more he believes in the possibility that what he saw was in some way alien, the further he is from the truth. I'm about to throw you to the wolves in the deep end of the pool that is also somehow on fire. You ready?"

She stared at the screen. "How do I start?"

Franklin's expression hardened and Athena got it, immediately. He was not going to hold her hand on this.

"Entirely up to you." He pursed his lips. "This is your case now. Yours. You call the shots. Let me know what resources you need and we'll make it happen. Within reason, of course. But, first, I need a plan. And I need it fast."

It was an awkward silence, until Athena nodded. "Understood," she said finally. "Ready to make it up as I go, sir."

Franklin's smile returned, but his eyes were still hard. "Enjoy the deep end of the pool." Franklin leaned back out of the cube and was gone. She heard him greet another of the Agents.

Athena sat at her desk, far away from the nearest window. She opened Mitchell Vincent's case file in front of her. She sighed, then opened her notebook. She twisted the head of a mechanical pencil, and got to work.

"Okay, Mr. Vincent," she said. "Let's tell a story."

— **2.4** —

The worn, pale yellow stuffed rabbit, whose name had changed no less that a dozen times before Allie finally settled on Mr. Rabbity Bunny, sat at the end of the table looming over a brightly-colored board game. A series of the game's cards were wedged into place in its large feet. Allie and Mitchell sat to its left, and Danielle to its right.

With a forceful series of bangs, Allie moved her blue token across the board. Each time she did, the pieces on the board rattled, and Mr. Rabbity Bunny threatened to topple over.

"One! Two! Three! Four! Five! Six!" she counted. She leaned back, and she studied the square where her piece landed in the same square as her father's. Allie let out a high-pitched burst of laughter. "Uh, oh, Daddy, you have to go all the way back to the start. So, so, sorry!"

Allie gleefully took Mitchell's colored token and placed it on the other side of the board in front of him.

"Hey," he shouted with mock indignity as his daughter giggled. "No fair!"

Danielle couldn't hold back the laughter. "Now, why would you do that to your Daddy?" she asked.

Allie gave them an exaggerated shrug. "Because that's the game. That's how you win! Your turn, Daddy. Then it's Mr. Rabbity Bunny's turn."

Mitchell picked up the dice and stared at them. He feigned confusion and turned to his daughter. "Okay, now, what do I do again?"

Allie rolled her eyes heavily. "You throw the dice, silly. And then you have to draw a card."

Mitchell shook the dice vigorously, and let them fly. "Okay, Bunny-bun. Here we go!"

The dice clattered on the board and revealed Mitchell's fate. He reached for his game piece and counted slowly for Allie as he moved it.

Danielle took Mitchell's hand and smiled at him and he smiled back. For the first time in a long time, she thought everything was going to be okay.

In the weeks to come, Danielle Vincent would find herself to proven be very, very wrong.

CHAPTER THREE
A RENDEZVOUS IN STARLIGHT

— 3.1 —

"Okay, let's talk about fact versus fiction," Cavanaugh said. She took a long, slow, breath in exasperation, and shook her head at Gerry Henry. She wanted very much to slap the smug grin and round glasses off his face. She'd listened to his nonsense long enough.

She gestured to the image on the screen, the ancient South American ruins of the ancient megalithic city of Pamapunku. Large stones interlocking thanks to precision mason work by the ancient Bolivians. It was a marvel of engineering, and would have taken them decades to build after the painstaking effort of moving the large stones to the mountaintop. Though, she would have to admit, it would have been much easier to build if they had used alien technology to do so.

Pamapunku was a poster child for alien construction. It was claimed that the stones at Pamapunku were cut to laser precision — a claim made a few moments ago by Gerry Henry as Mad Autumn flipped through the images of the ruins too fast for anyone to really get a good look at them. But even a precursory examination of the photographs on the screen showed they were clearly not. The work was an impressive achievement, but far from the levels of precision that were being attributed to them.

Henry then went on a five-minute extemporaneous tirade about a wild hypothesis using some kind of alien-made sonic technology to move the stones, complete with well-done concept art. Cavanaugh was still unclear how Henry came to this conclusion, but, the audience ate it up without question.

"About Pamapunku," she began, "to claim that it was made by alien technology is, if you'll forgive the expression, horse shit."

"Language!" Mad Autumn snapped with overly dramatic indignity, and the audience laughed. "There are alien children present!"

"Fine," Cavanaugh said. "It's grade-A horse crap."

Henry snorted, and took a drink from his bottled water. "A clear case of you manipulating the so-called facts," he said. He signaled to Mad Autumn. "Can you go back to the other slide? The one before?"

The image behind them switched to the tightly-fitted stones of the ruin in bright sunlight. "There's no way the ancient Bolivians could have built this site. It's just not possible. Those stones are granite! You can't just tool granite on this scale. It's not possible!"

"First of all, there is absolutely clear evidence of mason work," Cavanaugh said, "You can see it in the photo — drag marks on the stones, and imperfections everywhere at the site. You said that all of the stones are granite, and too hard to be cut by ancient tools, but more than ninety percent of them are much softer stone, sandstone and andesite, and much easier to work."

Mad Autumn checked her notes. "What's your source on that, Margret?"

"Margo," Cavanaugh corrected. "I don't know," she shrugged, "all credible archeologists? But if you were interested in facts, and not peddling your preconceived notions, maybe you'd acknowledge that. But, make up what you want, because why not?"

"Oh, come on," Henry waved her away. "It's right there! Ancient man was simply not capable of such feats. The only conclusion that anyone could make is that they had help."

The crowd gave him a gentle round of applause.

"From aliens," he added with a nod.

Pretending to show patience, Cavanaugh waited for the crowd to settle before she spoke. "This world is amazing," she said. "We, human beings, are amazing. You want to cheat our ancestors of their accomplishments by saying they had outside help? From aliens? You don't think that men, who are just as smart and capable as we are today, were unable to build monuments like Pamapunku, or the Pyramids? Why? Because that level of achievement is beyond man? Beyond their technology? It's simply not. Whether you like it or not, these structures were built by people. Not ancient alien technology, but by human beings. People like you and me. And that is far more incredible than what you're suggesting."

"It's certainly not credible," Henry said, "if that's what you mean."

Cavanaugh waved to Mad Autumn to move to the next topic. She was tired of beating her head against this particular block of stone.

With all the falsehoods flying around on the dais, Cavanaugh had to face one truth — this was going to be a long panel.

— 3.2 —

It was late. The offices of the Agency were dark except for the light of a desk lamp and computer monitor coming from a single cubicle.

Athena's.

Earlier in the day, she'd made her initial high-level presentation, put together a list of potential pieces of content to build her narrative, met with the other project leads for informal peer reviews, and broken the unofficial office policy and brought in a couple personal effects to decorate her office. Nothing extravagant, a photo of her and her father on a skiing trip, a few glass trophies — Addy's from her brief stint writing lawn mower commercials — and a stuffed rabbit, the exact same kind that Mitchell's kid called Mr. Rabbity. The research on Vincent's family the Agency had was impressive, and a bit terrifying.

She typed away on her computer, grinning with glee. Behind her, a plethora of multi-colored note cards, sticky-notes and printed pages were pinned to her cubicle wall with strings connecting various parts. She was, in essence, mapping out the conspiracy she expected Mitchell Vincent to follow.

She drank from a coffee mug shaped like an alien head that she found online. She spun around and checked the calendar on the wall. She circled a date in a few days' time with the hand-written note that read, 'Initial Contact.'

Athena startled when she heard Franklin's voice behind her. "You're working late."

To her, Franklin spontaneously appeared, lurking at the edge of her cubicle. He was still in his suit, though for the first time since she started at the Agency, his tie was loosened.

"I do that," she said. "I can't function without workohol." She raised her alien mug in salute. "Don't worry," she added, "It's just coffee."

"You *can* go home, you know," he said. He gestured to the other end of the building, with the badge checkpoint to get out.

"To what, exactly?" Athena asked. "Besides, when you have creative momentum, you respect it and keep moving forward."

"Fair enough," he said. "However, I've found that part of any good work-life balance is having some semblance of the latter."

"Then, why are you still here?"

"This is where I keep my workohol, too," he said. "Late night conference call with Arizona. Learn from my mistakes, Simms. Make sure you have some semblance of a life outside these walls." He knocked on the wall of her cubicle.

"I used to have a life, if you could call it that," she tossed the pencil onto a pile of notes, sketches and notecards. "Howard used to say I was only ever happy when I was working or drinking."

"Howard," Franklin raised an eyebrow. "Husband?"

"Ex," she corrected. "But Howard was wrong," she added darkly. "I was never really happy."

Franklin leaned against the wall of her cubicle, his eyes darting on the wall of notecards pinned to its walls.

"How long has it been?" he asked.

"Since I was married or since I've had a drink? Seven years for both." She thought about this. "I'm surprised there's anything about me you don't already know."

"People get unnerved, sometimes," he said, "when you know everything about them. I was being polite."

He was right, she thought. *It was unnerving.*

Athena turned back to her keyboard. "Work keeps me

focused. I just need to finish this thought." Franklin let her type away while he studied her board. A few moments later, she paused and took a deep breath.

She was, she had to admit, very pleased with herself.

"Making progress, I see." Franklin tapped one of the cards with a phrase in red marker. "What's this? 'Diner Encounter?' That wasn't in your initial outline."

"That's if he takes the bait." She waved to a set of cards at the far end of her work space. "The yellow cards are for if he doesn't. I think I've got the timeline all figured out. Spread out over about eight weeks, I'll need about twenty-seven pieces of content. Act One begins as soon as I can get this to Arizona."

She picked up a sealed, white envelope and offered it to the Director. "I'll need a little something extra for the next step," she said.

He took it from her and turned it over in his hands.

"Name it," Franklin said, "and it shall be yours."

She pointed to the 'Diner Encounter' card. "First of all, manpower."

Franklin plucked the Diner card from the wall and asked, "What exactly did you have in mind?"

"Two gentlemen, black suits, white shirts, black ties, square jaws, dark, menacing eyes," she said, excited. "I want them to look like they just walked straight out of *Reservoir Dogs*. And fedoras. Can I get fedoras?"

Franklin turned the card over in his hand. "I think we can make that happen. What do you want them to do, exactly?"

A flash of excitement crossed Athena's eyes. "I want them to scare the ever-loving hell out of Mr. Vincent."

— 3.3 —

Mitchell downed the last of his now cool coffee and headed towards the door at a quick pace. He wasn't running late, but he was on the cusp of it. His day-to-day life of insurance sales certainly wasn't the most exciting of lives, but it was his. He'd found a momentum in his work for the first time in weeks. And while sometimes tedious, Mitchell embraced the routine. Part of him found comfort in it. He grabbed his attaché bag, reached for the doorknob, and saw something he didn't expect. A plain, white envelope that appeared to have been slid under the door.

He called back to his wife, "I have to run."

"Have a good day, love," she said, but Mitchell didn't really hear the words.

Instead, he knelt down to examine the envelope and saw it had a message in a woman's handwriting and no return address. He picked it up, puzzling over what it might be. He froze when he saw what was scrawled on its front.

I need your help, it read.

His heart began to pound. His head whipped around, wondering if Danielle had seen it and hoping she hadn't. He instinctively hid it, sliding it into his inside jacket pocket. He didn't know what it was, but, it immediately put him on edge.

He heard the clank of a coffee mug being set on the kitchen counter, and Danielle stepped into view. With a wave of her arm, she shooed him away. "Don't be late. You don't want to get in trouble again."

"Don't worry." Mitchell smiled at his wife. "I'm not in that much trouble. It's been a good week so far."

"Then, one second," she said, quickly crossing the room to kiss him on the cheek. He impishly took her mug and took a drink before she snatched it back, letting out a warm laugh. "Go!"

But there was something in her eyes, he saw. A flash like she understood that something was wrong. He felt his cheeks flush.

Mitchell gave her a smile, but his mind was on the piece of paper in his pocket. His heart raced and he worried she had seen the letter. Worried she saw him sneak it into his jacket. Worried she had seen through him.

A few moments later, he was behind the wheel of his car. He whipped the envelope out of his jacket and inside found a simple note in Helvetica.

I know what you saw. You weren't the only one.
Be careful. They're watching you. We'll be in touch.

Mitchell's blood ran cold. He folded the paper, slowly.

"Everything's fine," he said. Then, as if to convince himself, he repeated it until it became a mantra.

"Everything's fine."

Mitchell opened the door, and made his way to his car.

"Everything's fine."

He put the key in the ignition.

"Everything's fine."

Every time he said it be became less and less convinced. His heart beat faster and faster. He put the car in gear and backed out of the driveway.

"Everything's fine."

He looked back to his house, his face twisted in worry.

"Everything's fine."

He pulled the car onto the highway and headed towards work.

"Everything's fine."

— 3.4 —

I know what you saw. You weren't the only one. Be careful. They're watching you. We'll be in touch.

All day, the words from the note gnawed at Mitchell. He couldn't focus throughout the day. He couldn't focus during the Anderson Account meeting. Not the stand up in the boss' office, or the call with headquarters in the afternoon. Not during playtime with Allie — coloring books with some rhinoceros character he couldn't remember the name of. Not through Spaghetti Thursday. Not while rewatching *The Next Generation* with Danielle for the umpteenth time.

I know what you saw. You weren't the only one. Be careful. They're watching you.

Not through small talk with Danielle. Not through his deflection of her questions of 'what's wrong.' Not through his lying in bed, unable to sleep. Not through his racing mind as the time ticked away in the seemingly endless night. He caught himself absently touching the scar on his temple, the thing he did when he was filled with nervous energy.

I know what you saw.

Then, from the nightstand, his cell rang. He snatched it before its vibrations could awaken Danielle. The number was unknown, so he sent it to voicemail. Part of him knew — perhaps some kind of premonition — that it was connected to the note he received this morning.

When he played the voicemail, he was proven right.

"You got my note?" the panicked voice of a woman said in hushed tones. "You're not alone, I saw it too. I can't talk long. This line might not be secure. If you want to know the truth, and, if you can, meet me at the Starlight Diner on Route Five in exactly one hour."

The call went dead and Mitchell stared at the phone. Mitchell's wife rolled over, half-awake.

"Whazzat," she mumbled.

"Nothing. Nobody. Go back to sleep, honey," he said, then listened to the message again.

You weren't the only one.

He sat up on the edge of the bed, staring into the darkness of the room. Behind him, Danielle rolled, and a second later, she was completely dead to the world.

Mitchell held his phone to his ear and listened to the message again and again. He didn't know this woman. But if she saw it too, he had to know what she knew. He had to know he wasn't the only one. He had to know he hadn't lost his mind. He had to know he was right.

Be careful.

But he'd promised Danielle he'd let it go. Promised he'd stay off the forums. Promised he'd stay off of the internet endlessly scrolling through videos of alien sightings. Promised he'd put her and Allie first.

But the woman sounded like she needed help. Like she was in trouble. Like there were people after her. He had to help, didn't he?

They're watching you.

He did the math in his head, and tried to talk himself out of it. He waited until he would be ten minutes late to his rendezvous at the diner before he steeled himself, and finally made a decision.

— **3.5** —

The Starlight Diner's neon sign shone in the night with a shooting star blinking above the words '24 Hours.' Mitchell's car pulled up to the parking lot just in time to see another car, a small, gray hatchback speed away, kicking the gravel of the parking lot as it swerved onto the road. Whoever it was, they were in a hurry. Part of him wondered if he should follow it. If that could have been the woman on the other end of the phone. But, he didn't get a chance to see the driver. He rolled to a stop, his eyes scanning the area. There were only three other cars in the lot other than his. Two were parked on the edge of the lot, and probably worked the night shift. The other was a large, black sedan.

Immediately after the car that had peeled out of the parking lot rounded the corner out of sight, two men in dark suits and fedoras raced out of the diner and scrambled into the black sedan, which he guessed was an unmarked police car. Seconds later, the sedan was in hot pursuit. It streaked out of the parking lot and took off in the direction of the hatchback.

If his heart wasn't pounding before, it was thundering now. He put the car in park, watched their taillights vanish in the night, and wondered what to do.

He peered into the diner itself, he only saw a lone waitress behind the counter, staring intently at her phone. He knew he should go home immediately. He should forget what he saw. He should delete the video. Delete his account from the forums. Delete his emails about it.

Instead, he got out of his car and carefully walked to

the diner. He kept one eye on the road, just in case those two men with the definite detective vibe decided to come back.

I know what you saw. You weren't the only one. Be careful. They're watching you.

Whoever this woman was, in her voicemail she sounded scared. He had to find out everything he could. The door rang with a bell, the waitress, a young, pretty woman with dark hair, glanced up from her phone.

Mitchell entered the diner cautiously. He nodded to the young woman in the waitress smock and sat at the counter. The waitress leaned in and took out her pad. The man in the kitchen raised his spatula in greeting.

"What was that about?" he asked, trying not to sound nervous, and not at all confident he was doing so.

The young woman shrugged. "Not sure," she said. "This woman was sitting by herself and bugged out when these two government-suit-types showed up. One of them was pretty handsome. She must've crawled out the bathroom window."

Mitchell tried to sound casual. He had no idea whether or not he was succeeding. "What did she look like?"

"Mousy. Glasses. Average. Nervous. Ordered a coffee and put way too much sugar in it, not that I'm judging." The waitress leaned in and added a bit of a sultry husk to her voice. "You her lover?" she asked, letting her 'r' roll.

Mitchell was taken aback. "What?"

"She was waiting for someone. That someone you? Yeah. It was you." She eyed him up and down, and said just above a whisper. "Is this your first time cheating?"

"Excuse me?"

She tapped the wedding band on his hand with her pen. "You're wearing a wedding ring. She wasn't. If you're going to do this, you gotta pay attention to the details," she said.

"It's not that," Mitchell assured her. He must have come across as nervous.

"It's okay," she said, raising her hands in apology. "I don't judge. Hell, if my husband knew half of what I did," she trailed off with a chuckle. "She in trouble? Who were those men? What did they want?"

Mitchell shook his head. "I don't know."

The waitress studied him. "Are you in some kind of trouble, mister?"

"I don't know."

"You don't know much, do you, Mitchell?" she said.

Mitchell was about to say 'no,' when her words caught up with him. His back tensed. He eyed her carefully. "How did you know my name?" he asked.

The waitress cleared her throat and pointed her pen to the booth in the corner. "She was sitting over there, lover boy."

Mitchell followed the waitress' gaze to a booth at the far corner of the diner. She shooed him along, and he made his way to the booth. "Can I get you anything?" she called.

"Not right now," he said.

"You know, if you don't order anything, I don't get tipped. Randy back there doesn't get tipped." She pointed her pen to the man in the back looming over the grill. "Randy and I like getting tipped."

"Give me a minute, then," he said. As he sat down at the booth and saw something poking out from underneath the placemat. He tugged at it, and pulled out another white envelope. He turned it over in his hands, and saw his name written on it in a woman's handwriting. It was the same handwriting from the envelope left at his house.

She left this for him. Mitchell raised an eyebrow at the waitress, still behind the counter.

"I peeked," she said. "Sorry."

Mitchell ripped the envelope open and pulled out a folded piece of paper. It was a badly xeroxed copy of a memo that had been streaked with a marker with several blocks of words blacked out. The memo had a relatively fresh coffee stain in the lower corner. His eyes skimmed the document to focus on the few words that he could make out.

Testing.

Hadron.

Prototype.

Reverse-engineered.

And a word that he could make out that was only partially blacked out. *Alien.* At the top of the document he saw a logo seal with a bird with its wings spread that read in bold letters, *Project: Carolina.*

"Carolina?" he whispered aloud, unaware that the waitress was right behind him. He'd been so focused, he didn't see it when the waitress slid into the booth opposite him.

"That her name? Caroline?" She saw the paper in his hand, but clearly not the content. The black marker lines would clearly have given it away for what it was. A secret. Mitchell quickly folded the paper and put it away.

"Dear John letter, ain't it?" she asked. "Sorry, hon. Happens to the best of us. I mean, at least it wasn't by breakup-by-text, am I right?" '

"I'd appreciate you minding your own business," he said.

"Not really my style," she admitted. "I haven't seen your wife, but, you probably could do better than Caroline."

Headlights panned across the diner, and Mitchell heard the sound of the crunch of tires on gravel. The black sedan had returned.

"Appears your buddies are back," the waitress said.

Mitchell looked out the window to see a man in a black suit, white shirt and black tie, getting out of the black sedan. The man stepped with his hands behind his back, in a military at-ease position. He was a broad, fit man, about to burst out of his suit. Another man got out of the passenger side. He wore a similar dark suit, leaned against Mitchell's car, and crossed his arms.

Mitchell swallowed. He took the document, and slid it under the table. He tried, as nonchalantly as he could manage, to slide the folded paper down inside his pants.

"You sure you're not in trouble, hon?" the waitress asked with a hint of worry in her voice.

"Everything's fine," he said, but he didn't believe it.

And he wasn't sure she believed him either.

The larger man adjusted his fedora, and stared directly at Mitchell through the window. Mitchell thought the man might have tipped his hat to him.

With a wave of a finger, the man motioned for Mitchell to come outside.

"Should I call the cops?" she asked. "Or are they the cops?"

"I'm going to find out." Mitchell got up, forcing himself to put one foot in front of the other. When the door to the Starlight opened, the man again motioned for Mitchell to come closer.

Mitchell froze.

The man called to Mitchell, "Evening, sir. Can I have a moment of your time, please?"

"That's my car," he managed. "If you'll excuse me, I have to get home."

"I understand that," the man said, "but, I think we should have a little talk first. I promise it'll only take a moment."

"Can I help you?" It took everything Mitchell had to keep himself from running. He tried to assure himself that they wouldn't possibly do anything, there were two witnesses in the diner.

That's what he told himself, anyway.

"That's why I'm here," the man said. "I understand you saw something last week. Let's call it an 'event.' And I understand you have video of the event."

Mitchell turned to the other man leaning against his

car. The man, smaller than his partner, glared at him with his arms deep in his pockets.

Mitchell steeled himself and turned to the larger man in front of him. "If that were true," he said, "I'd be very interested in how you know that, sir."

"Well," he said, taking a step closer and causing Mitchell to flinch, "let's just say, that while you were watching the event, someone was watching *you*."

Mitchell felt his knees weaken, but he summoned all the strength he had. "Who are you? I want to see some ID," he demanded, but the other man's eyes narrowed..

"Oh, we're not going to give you that," he said.

"Why not?" Mitchell asked.

"Because, I don't exist," he said. He nodded to his partner. "Neither does he. And I am coming to believe you don't quite understand the severity our little situation, Mitchell Vincent."

"I have a right to know who I'm talking to."

"Sure about that, are you?"

"I don't know what's going on. Am I being detained?" he asked.

"First, we're not police." The smaller man leaning against Mitchell's car gave him an unnerving half-smile. "This is a just a polite conversation between three new acquaintances."

"Then, I'm leaving." Mitchell moved towards the man. With all his courage, he added, "Get off my car."

The smaller man raised his brow at his partner, as if asking permission. The larger man nodded. The smaller man straightened, adjusted his tie, and pushed himself off of Mitchell's car. He casually strode away. As soon as the man was clear, Mitchell threw the door open, and fumbled getting the key into the ignition.

"You want some free advice?" the larger man approached him, and leaned down to the window. "I'd forget what you saw. I'd take everything down from those forums you like. Delete everything from your phone; your computer. And if I were to get a call from a strange woman in the middle of night, I'd ignore it. For your own wellbeing, Mr. Vincent. And for your family's. For little Allie, and Danielle."

Mitchell stiffened at the sound of his family's names. "You're not me. You don't tell me what to do. You don't know me."

Mitchell got into his car and slammed the door. The smaller man leaned in to the window, and for the first time, spoke.

"We're getting to, though," the smaller man said. "And that's fun."

His partner added, "And just so you know, this conversation is far from over. Oh, and tell your friend, Gemini, that we're watching her, too."

Gemini, Mitchell thought. *Was that her name? Some kind of codename?*

With that, the smaller man moved away from the car, and Mitchell cranked the engine. He slammed his foot on the accelerator and sped away as fast as he could. His breath came out in sharp bursts, as his let out a shout of both fear and victory that he had gotten out of that without a fight.

Without jail.

Or worse.

Every few seconds he checked the rearview mirror to make sure the men weren't following him. They knew his name. They knew what he had seen. They knew the username of the person that contacted him.

He wiped the sweat from his brow, knowing it would be hours before he'd be able to get to sleep.

If at all.

— 3.6 —

Athena waited on the side of the road. She didn't know how long it would be before Agents Howell and Osbourne would arrive at the designated mile marker for the post-op rendezvous. If everything had gone according to plan, after she peeled out of the diner parking lot, Howell and Osbourne would have doubled back to confront Mr. Vincent, and dropped enough hints to make him think he had been on to something with his video.

A bit of classic reverse psychology.

Every time a set of headlights rounded the bend in the road, she tensed up, expecting to see the black sedan with her two fedora-wearing agents in it. They looked perfect. Howell was square-jawed, broad and intimidating. He was grim and far too serious. Throughout the mission briefings and the time spent workshopping the encounter in an empty conference room leading up to tonight, Athena wasn't sure she had ever seen the man smile. She found him either extremely professional to a fault, or lacked any kind of personality whatsoever. However, he was, in Athena's humble opinion, just stupidly handsome. She would make it her mission to get him to smile, even if it killed her.

The other Agent, Osbourne, was lean, with menacing hooded eyes. Unlike his counterpart, Osbourne was jovial, friendly, and surprisingly good at the improv exercises she had conducted. He was quick-witted, and funny, but as they developed the encounter with Mitchell Vincent, she found him far more effective and threatening just glaring silently. If he could keep from grinning, that was.

When the black sedan finally pulled in behind her, Athena threw open the door and couldn't contain her excitement. She couldn't tell from Howell's expression if it had gone poorly, if he was still in character, or if he was his usually grim self. Osbourne, however, was all smiles.

"He took the bait?" Athena asked.

"That's a yes. I think I saw him stuff something in his pants," Osbourne said.

"We double-checked the booth, and did not find the package," Howell added. "The waitress was very interested in the situation."

"And Vincent?" Athena asked.

"Mission accomplished. Mr. Vincent attempted to appear tough," Howell said. "He was not effective. We suggested very strongly that he should forget what he saw. I expect he will not."

"Consider Mr. Vincent scared out of his wits, boss. He's spooked." Osbourne slapped Howell on the shoulder. "This guy," he added, "I didn't know he had it in him. He was great. I mean, he's off to do Hamlet next."

"Do I detect a new career?" Athena asked. "The next Olivier or Branagh, perhaps? Come on, smile for me, Howell."

Howell let out a sigh under his breath, but, Athena noted, did not smile. "I think not," he said.

"Fantastic," Athena grinned. "Just fantastic. You guys are amazing."

"Scaring him was easy," Osbourne, said. "He was shaking."

"But it's not like he's in any real danger," Athena waved a dismissive hand, then threw her hand to her forehead in an overly dramatic swoon. "This is just *theater.*"

This drew no reaction from Howell, much to Athena's disappointment.

"What now, boss?" he asked.

"Now?" Athena said. "We wait to see what he does next and we adjust the narrative accordingly."

— 3.7 —

Sweating, exhausted, and still feeling the nauseous twinge of the adrenaline rush from the Starlight, Mitchell collapsed into his home office chair. *Who were those men? What did they want? Who, or what, is Carolina? Who was that woman?*

The questions raced through his mind, colliding with one another until they blurred into one singular question.

What was going on?

He had driven aimlessly from the diner until he was certain he wasn't being followed. But if they knew his name, and the names of his wife and child, they probably knew where he lived. He tried not to let the dread overtake him. *Did they have access to his phone? How did they know he'd been contacted? Had they read his forum posts?*

He had pulled the envelope from his pants, and it sat next to him on the ride home. It was a little worse for wear, crinkled around the edges, but still intact. He flicked on his desk lamp and unfolded the paper.

Mitchell's office desk was forced against the wall between two overstuffed bookshelves. On his desk there were a series of toys from his youth — among them, an original Megatron that turned into a Walther handgun and a ceramic Darth Vader piggy bank. He sat in a lounge chair, with the redacted document in his hand.

He heard the creak of a floorboard and a long, high-pitched yawn coming from the hallways. Mitchell instinctively folded the document, and turned to the doorway to see Danielle shuffling into the room.

"What's going on?" Danielle asked just above a whisper. "I woke up and you weren't there. You okay?"

She entered the office and patted him on the shoulder. He reached up to take her hand, only to realize how sweaty his hands felt.

"Sorry, honey, I couldn't sleep." Mitchell gave her hand one last pat before pulling his own away and wiping it on his pants. "Yeah, everything's fine. I'm just a little off. It's been a while since I took my pills, and my body is still adjusting. I'll be to bed soon."

"Okay, baby," she said, and leaned down to kiss him on the forehead. "Don't stay up too late. You need to sleep."

"I know," he said. "Go back to bed."

She stroked his shoulder and turned back to the door. Danielle plodded off, stifling another mighty yawn.

As soon as she was out of sight, Mitchell got up and slowly closed the office door. Once he heard the click of the latch, he returned to his desk. He carefully unfolded the document and studied it. He read it, and reread it. With as much of it redacted, he could only make out little more than sentence fragments. He could tell there were two blocks of words that must have been identical, because they were the same length. A seal in the upper corner was that of an eagle with the words circling it blacked out — a logo he was not familiar with. A watermark of the word 'classified,' repeated in a diagonal pattern, filling the page. But he could glean some things from what could be read between the streaks of black marker.

He scanned it, and started to make notes. The project, whatever it was, was code-named 'Carolina.' There was a hint of whatever it was being reverse-engineered from another piece of technology, possibly extraterrestrial. A sloppily-redacted word could have been 'propulsion.'

The other thing he noted was the page was not an original, but a photocopy stained with a circular ring of coffee. Mitchell felt the excitement fade, and the weight of his own exhaustion. Despite what had happened, he caught himself nodding off in his chair. He estimated he could still be able to get a few hours' sleep before he took his file and uploaded it to the 'Strange Sightings' forum in a new discussion thread.

His fingers flew over the screen.

This was dropped in my lap, he typed. *Literally. Has something to do with my video. Has anyone ever heard of Project: Carolina?*

Mitchell leaned back, took a deep breath and hit 'enter.'

He stared at the alert icon in the upper right corner of the webpage signaling a response. He didn't have to wait long. A few moments later, the site gave a satisfying bing and the number one appeared next to his alert counter.

Mitchell clicked immediately to see a message that read, *I see that you made it home safely. I'm so glad.*

The username read '*Geminii_22.*'

Mitchell stared at it in disbelief. He clicked the name and scrolled through the user's page, but found no real information. They were not one of the regulars that he occasionally chatted or sparred with in the forums. A fresh wave of panic and excitement hit him. Mitchell typed furiously.

Who is this?

The cascading dots indicating that someone was typing flickered in the chat window, then, a new message appeared, again from the *Geminii_22* user.

A friend. Will be in touch soon. Have to go. Then, a few

moments later, a simple, ominous message appeared.

But be careful. They monitor us. Always.

Mitchell closed his browser window, and leaned back in his chair, worried. Suddenly finding his energy renewed, he spent the next few hours scrolling through the forums, searching for anything that might be connected. But everything led to more worry. More questions that ultimately boiled down the singular thought on his mind.

What was going on?

It was almost five when he tried to crawl back into bed. Danielle shifted as he slid under the covers. He stared at the ceiling until the exhaustion of the night caught up to him.

A few attempted hours of fitful sleep, he decided, were better than none at all.

CHAPTER FOUR

WATER FOR THE ROSE

— 4.1 —

The gods and stars looked down upon the Mayan King Pakal descending into the open maw of the Underworld. He sank beneath the World Tree of his people and he stared up at a great bird-like beast called Wuqub'Kaqix. The roots of the World Tree encircled him, and his body rested on the head of a celestial serpent as he reached for the heavens.

At least, this is what Cavanaugh saw in the intricately-carved relief sculpture on the lid of his sarcophagus. The King had been buried in a pyramid known as the Temple of the Inscriptions, and was widely thought to be a representation of his transition into divinity, similar to other carvings elsewhere in the temple.

A rumble moved through the modest convention crowd. Cavanaugh knew what she was about to say would enrage the other panelists on the dais. She shook her head and turned to the man with the round glasses on her right.

"Sorry, Gerry," she said. "I just don't see it."

Gerry Henry fumed. He stood and pointed to the drawing on the screen. "Go to annotated slide, Maddy," he snapped to Mad Autumn.

Mad Autumn jumped when Henry yelled. Cavanaugh could tell she was caught off guard. Mad Autumn pressed the button on her controller, and the image of the carving now had red outlines that made the various elements of the design connect in a way that superficially appeared to be a space capsule.

"How," he pointed to the rocket shape outlined in red. "How can you look at that and not see a rocket ship? How could it be any more obvious that that's what it is?"

Cavanaugh had to admit, if one turned the image sideways, and if someone were to selectively connect the elements of the stylized design of the sarcophagus, and to arbitrarily say the image at the bottom was fire, it might look like a rocket ship. It also might look like the position of his hands and feet were not the image of him falling, or as some believed, in a position representing childbirth connected to his rebirth as a god, but instead were seen as operating some kind of control system.

But to see that, it would mean ignoring the context of

the surrounding artwork in the pyramid, and the complex symbology of Mayan myth. And that's exactly what Henry and apparently every other person in the room wanted to do.

"Oh, I don't know," Cavanaugh said with a dismissive shrug, "probably because it's entirely consistent with other burial images from the ancient Mayans? This is far more likely a depiction of Pakal's descent into the Underworld than it is of a singular example of a man in a space ship. That rocket casing is a pretty common depiction of their 'World Tree' concept. Your 'rocket exhaust' is just the roots of the tree."

"Unbelievable," Henry snorted.

"Yes," Cavanaugh said. "I agree."

Henry threw his hands in the air, making a good show for the crowd. Cavanaugh had to wonder how much of his theatrics were for their benefit, and not really reflective of his actual beliefs.

Was he a believer? she asked herself. *Or was this all for show?*

Henry made his living as an extraterrestrial expert. Appearing on aliens shows, speaking at conventions, not to mention his own lucrative series of 'non-fiction' books. He was charismatic, and, good with a crowd.

"There's tons of evidence of aliens all throughout South American history," Henry said. "From Bolivia, to megalithic structures beyond the capabilities of human hands, to the Nazca Lines that can only be seen from the sky. You can't just summarily dismiss all of it."

"Pretty sure I can," Cavanaugh said with confidence.

"Especially when all you have is selective examples and ad hoc evidence."

"So you don't give any credence to alien influence on ancient South America," Henry said.

She waved to the image on the screen of the ancient god in his 'rocket ship.' "You'll have to come up with better evidence than it-kind-of-sort-of-looks-like-a-rocket-if-you-squint-at-it," she said.

She turned to the audience as someone actually booed. Others in the crowd just laughed.

"What about Machu Picchu?" he asked.

"Changing the subject as a debate tactic, then. Got it," Cavanaugh sighed. "Okay, I'll bite. What about Machu Picchu?"

"Machu Picchu could not have been built by humans," he said. "Can we go to that slide please, darling?" Annoyed, Henry signaled to Mad Autumn and she scrolled through the next few slides highlighting various sections of Pakal relief to a photo of a stone city among the Peruvian mountains.

Henry retook his seat on the dais. "How could ancient Peruvians possibly have built that — just *look* at it! — without external help? How could they possibly have moved all that stone with the technology at hand?"

"If I had to guess, it's more likely they did it the same way the ancient Egyptians moved giant stones, with rolling logs, than to say it was extraterrestrial influence."

Gerry Henry relaxed. He took his glasses off and polished the lenses with a small cloth. He gave her a self-satisfied smile. "Come on, now. We all know trees don't grow at that altitude, so you can't use the rolling log theory to explain how they built Machu Picchu." Henry scoffed. "The stone they used isn't native to the region, and there's no evidence that they were quarried. They didn't have the technology to either cut or move stone of that size."

"So, you're perfectly willing to believe that they transported hundreds of multi-ton stones from one region to the other with some kind of alien device, but the idea that they couldn't also transport logs to the region to use the rolling method is completely out of the question? You realize how that sounds?"

"Sounds like someone is in denial about the evidence," Henry said, and the convention hall crowd laughed.

"Yeah, it does," Cavanaugh said with more than a hint of snark. "Also, despite the overwhelming evidence that these stones were, in fact, quarried and moved, you just, what? Ignore that? Because, aliens? It's more ad hoc rationalization, ignoring evidence because it doesn't conform with a pre-determined conclusion."

Mad Autumn asked, "Are you suggesting that Dr. Henry just sees what he wants to see?"

Cavanaugh leaned back in her chair. "Doesn't everyone?"

— 4.2 —

"You wanted to see me?" Athena announced her presence with a gentle knock on the door frame to Director Franklin's office. She was still jet lagged from the flight back from Arizona, and had not had sufficient coffee.

"You took an unnecessary risk at the Starlight, Simms," Franklin waved her in. He stood in front of one of his conspiracy boards, and was in the middle of moving bits of information from one column that read, 'Passive' to another that read, 'Active.' He spun around to her. "I inferred from your briefing that your team members would be the only ones actually on site. You really shouldn't have put yourself in the field like that. You're not trained for it."

Athena had prepared herself for this. "I wanted to be an actress," she said. "But, I was told I wasn't leading lady material. So, if I wanted to act, I had to write parts for myself. I was a playwright before I was a novelist, you know."

"Ah," Franklin's eyes went up as he was lost in thought, "one of your early works. *The February Man,* a thinly-veiled variant on Frankenstein."

Athena frowned. She hadn't thought about that play in years.

Franklin continued, "Ran two weeks at your college theater where you played the lead. A scientist tampering with forces beyond her control, questions of morality, playing god and losing. I read it."

"You read it?" she asked, unsure that a manuscript even

still existed. Athena felt a twinge of uncomfortableness at Franklin's knowledge of her work. She shook it off.

"I skimmed it, to be honest," Franklin shrugged. "You've gotten much better since then. It was a bit clunky in the second act, and I can't imagine that anyone in the audience wouldn't have been ahead of the plot."

"Fair," she said. "How do you remember all this?"

"I have a peculiar memory," Franklin said. "It's useful in this line of work. There's a lot to see in the thirty-thousand-foot view. Now, about the Starlight Diner incident. I read Howell's report."

Athena took one of the seats in the office. "I think I can handle some light improv with a waitress in the middle of nowhere."

Franklin picked up a memo from his desk, his eyes scanned it. "I'm not particularly worried about some random waitress, Penny Williams, of 415 Roland Drive, Apartment B, Middle of Nowhere, Arizona," he said. "I'm worried that you will consider this is a precedent for further engagement."

She pursed her lips. "I understand. However, you said I can run this however I see fit," she reminded him. "Do I have that autonomy?"

"You do," Franklin said after the briefest of hesitations.

"Good," she said, but before she could continue, Franklin raised a halting finger.

"But," he said, "it's unwise to engage personally. You need to keep a certain distance to keep objectivity from your target. This is not just for your physical safety, but for your emotional safety as well. These are the words of experience, I assure you."

"Understood. And you had said I can have whatever I need?" she asked, then, quickly added, "within reason of course."

Franklin nodded for her to continue.

"I need someone who can design alien hieroglyphs and star charts and an expert in astrophysics who can do some, shall we say, weird calculations for me."

A smile spread across Franklin's face. "And you shall have them."

Franklin picked up a rotating file and flipped through the contact cards rapidly. The analog nature of this pleased her. He hummed as he searched, but she didn't recognize the tune. A few seconds later, he plucked a card and offered it to her while still scrolling through the file

"Here's a graphic designer in Osaka who knows how to keep his mouth shut," he said. "He's great at left-of-center projects like this one. We use a phony video game company as a front to do requests like this. Make up something about this being part of a concept art package or something."

"Really?"

"Lots of games never make it out of the concept phase, so, it never getting produced will be good cover." Franklin continued to rifle through his contacts. "His English is decent, but be sure to communicate in simple sentences. Do it on our secure video chat. Don't put anything in an email to him unless you absolutely, absolutely have to."

"The goal is no paper trail," she repeated the thing that

Franklin had drilled into her over the last few weeks.

"An admirable, yet impossible goal." Franklin plucked another card from his file. This one had a business card stapled to it. He offered it to Athena.

"Here's a professor in a small Cali college who we've used on more than a few occasions. Victoria is used to 'interesting requests,'" he said. "We usually tell her it's research for a screenplay. She *loves* that."

"I assume you can trust them," Athena asked.

"I trust them to fear the consequences of their non-compliance," he said.

Athena raised an eyebrow at that.

"Oh, it's nothing like that," he said. "But the non-disclosure agreements we've set up with them are pretty iron-clad, and we pay them enough for them to not ask too many questions."

"Right," she said. "I also need to fake some documents for a big company that has done military contracts. Like a Boeing or a Haliburton, anything like that? The more well-known the better."

Franklin snapped his fingers. "Glowaski International," he said. "They make everything from military aircraft to theme park ride vehicles. We have a long-standing arrangement. I can even get you access to their document templates."

"Wait!" The news excited Athena. "Can we put something on their site? Like a project archive?"

"We should be able to make something like that happen," he said. "I'll get you in touch with someone in tech."

"How long have they been around?" She flicked the cards in her hand.

"Since the mid-sixties, I think," Franklin said.

"Hm," Athena thought about it. "I would have preferred something that's been around since at least Roswell."

Franklin laughed.

"Rookie mistake," he said. "Can't go to the Roz-well too often."

Athena didn't bother to hide her disappointment. "I see."

"Your instincts are right, though," he said, "to tie this to an event the past. Just steer clear of July '47. Too much is already hitched to that post, if you know what I mean. There are a lot of other incidents to mine, though."

"Got it!" she said. She slapped the two cards together, thinking. The possibilities flooded her.

"You're doing good work here, Simms," he said. She must have been smiling when Franklin patted her shoulder. "Keep it up."

"I intend to, boss," she beamed. "Now, if you'll excuse me, I have a story to tell."

— 4.3 —

Danielle Vincent didn't know what to do. No idea what she should do. She laid awake, eyes closed. She could only guess how late it was. Beside her, she felt Mitchell toss and turn. Occasionally, he would whisper to himself, but she could never quite make out what he was saying. He'd been doing this almost every night for the last week. Since, she realized, that night she found him unable to sleep in his office.

Over the last week, she'd tried to talk to him. Tried to engage him, but he kept pulling further and further away. Something had happened to him, she was sure of that. She tried to tell herself that it was nothing. That he was worried about work. But her imagination was getting the better of her.

Mitchell had promised he would let it go, but he'd spent almost every evening in his office with the door closed. Tonight, all night long, she'd listened to his printer humming. He'd only stepped out of his office to use the bathroom, and even took his dinner in there while she and Allie ate by themselves. Allie had been worried, asking if Daddy was sick. Danielle tried to assure her that he was just working.

It was after midnight when she had knocked on the door, asking him to come to bed, and it was nearly an hour later when he actually did.

When he crawled into bed, she pretended to sleep, her mind oscillating between anger and despair. After nearly two hours of fitful sleep, Mitchell sat up. She felt Mitchell ease himself out of bed, as he had done almost every night for the last week. She felt him lean over her and give her a kiss on the cheek. She didn't stir. She didn't respond. She remained as still as she could.

It wasn't until she heard the front door open and close and the car start did she get up. She tried the door to his office, and found it locked. Dread crept through her as she made her way to the living room window and pulled back the curtains.

She watched as Mitchell's car pulled away, only turning on its lights when it got a clear of the curb and well down the road a few dozen yards away. She had no idea where he was going, but, there was no answer she could think of that would be good news.

Danielle was furious. And scared. And most of all, worried about her husband.

— 4.4 —

It was a bright, sunny morning, and Athena was in an excellent mood. She made her way to the front of the Agency office building, swiping her badge on the black sensor on the side of the unassuming office door. The sensor beeped and there was a satisfying clunk as the door unlocked.

Trying to the navigate the handle with a latte in hand, she got it just open enough to get her foot in and swung it the rest of the way open. She passed Melody at the reception desk who sat in front of a highly-detailed map of the moon. She headed up the stairs to the second level, and to the second security checkpoint. A second badge swipe, a second beep, and a second satisfying clunk as the door unlocked.

With a bit of a bounce in her step, she waved to the other agents she passed. Dunham on 'Operation Bluewater.' Lee on 'Fidget.' Finch on 'Nessie.' They smiled at her as she passed, her peers in the weird. She waved at Franklin when she passed his office and he was on the phone assuring someone, a congressman from what little she heard of it, that everything was under control. Franklin waved back, but continued with his call. She wondered which of the projects he was referring to, or if it was something she was not even aware of.

When she got to her cubicle, she found Agent Howell sitting at her desk, scrolling through something on his phone. He looked up at her, rose from the seat, and straightened his jacket.

"Morning, boss," he said, offering her own seat to her.

"To what do I owe the pleasure of a gentleman caller?" she asked. Try as she might, she had yet to even get Howell to crack a smile.

"I wanted to update you on a development last night," he said. "It's in the morning briefing to Director Franklin, but I thought you should see it, too. Vincent was sighted outside the Arizona complex last night."

Howell turned his phone over to Athena for her to see a grainy, black-and-white still image of man sitting on the hood of a car with his head craned up at the skies overhead.

It was unmistakably Mitchell Vincent.

Mitchell sat on the parked car in the same spot where he first shot footage of the strange aircraft, his phone in his hand. He stared at the stars above, as if waiting for anything.

"Security footage caught Vincent outside the testing area last night at 1:00 a.m.," Howell reported. "He stayed there for just under three hours and, then, drove home. He published a three thousand word diatribe about what he saw, Carolina, his experiences. The forums went berserk. We're at hundreds of comments. It sparked a video essay on YouTube that is on track to hit ten thousand views in the next three hours. His posts about Carolina are starting to get momentum."

"Wow," she said. "Can you print that for me?"

Howell quickly tapped his phone. A few seconds later, she heard the printer in the hallway spring to life.

Athena made a note on a three-by-five card and pinned it to the conspiracy board. She checked her spreadsheet timeline, and made a note on the calendar pinned to the wall of her cubicle.

"We're getting traction ahead of schedule." She checked her calendar. "If the fish is hooked, then maybe it's time to reel him in. Can we be set for the Rosewater tonight?"

"About that. He hasn't actually seen you yet," Howell said. "We should use an Operative with more undercover experience to handle this, to pretend to be Gemini."

Athena waved her hand as if to shoo away the notion.

"I've been through this with Franklin. Mitchell Vincent has a history of obsessive-compulsive behavior and fringe thinking, but not violence. There's no indication that he's any kind of a threat. The risk should be minimal."

"Still," Howell said. "I'd prefer you not do this personally."

"*You'd* prefer," Athena said. "Do I detect some manner of camaraderie from you, Smiles?"

Howell's jaw clenched whenever she called him that.

"It's for your own safety," he said. "And your personal security is part of my purview. In the past, Director Franklin has only allowed properly trained Field Agents to handle such things. However, if you're going to insist…"

"I am," she confirmed. "I don't want anyone else making things up I can't anticipate or work into the narrative later. I know the project better than anybody. Don't worry, Smiles, I'll be able to lead him where I need him to go."

Howell stiffened, his eyes locked onto hers. "So, it's about ego, then."

That hit her like a slap in the face. "It's about the best way to accomplish the mission," she countered.

"I'll be on site if there's any trouble," Howell said. "Just in case."

"Won't he recognize you?" she gestured at his frame. "You don't exactly blend into the background, you and your shoulders."

"I'll stay out of sight," Howell assured her. "Don't worry about me."

Athena eyed him up and down. "Are you physically capable of not wearing a black suit?"

Howell shrugged, then cracked the barest hint of a smile. "First time for everything, I suppose."

That smile brought Athena Simms great joy.

— 4.5 —

When the phone rang, Danielle tensed. They'd only kept the land-line for emergencies, but she couldn't remember anyone other than her mother who had called her on that number in months. She checked the ID on the wireless receiver, and let this Unknown Caller go to voicemail. With Mitchell locked in his office, again, and Allie in bed, Danielle was feeling very alone in the house.

She tried to draw Mitchell out of his dark cave twice, but no luck, and had been scrolling endlessly online trying to distract herself from the anxiety building in her since.

The phone rang again, still listing Unknown Caller. She checked the phone's docking base. Where there would have been a blinking light indicating a message, there was nothing. Annoyed, Danielle sent it back to voicemail.

A few moments later, the phone rang for a third time. She stared at the receiver, and clicked the green button.

"Vincents," she answered.

"Is Mitchell there? His cell must be off," a woman's

voice asked. She sounded out of breath, with a hint of panic in her voice. "It's urgent that I speak to him."

Danielle didn't recognize the woman's voice. "Who is this?"

"This is, uh, Mary from the office," the woman said.

"Mary, is it?" Danielle couldn't remember a single instance of anyone from work calling on their home phone. She stared at the hallway leading to Mitchell's office. Whoever this woman was, Danielle assumed that every word she was going to say was going to be a lie.

"Yes," 'Mary' answered.

"Uh, huh. One moment." Danielle took the phone to Mitchell's office and gave it a tentative knock. "Mitchell," she called through the door. "It's Mary from the office. Who's 'Mary from the office?'"

She heard the squeak of the knob turning. The door cracked open and Mitchell peeked out, blocking her from seeing what was inside. The room was filled with shadow. The windows were closed and the only light in the room was the glow of his computer. The monitor and his desk had been turned away from the door, so that she couldn't see the screen.

"She's new," he said, which may have been the most blatant lie Danielle had ever heard from her husband. The expression on his face told her that he had no idea who this person was. If there was a Mary from the office, he'd never mentioned her.

Danielle pushed herself into the doorway before handing him the phone. Mitchell tried to hide his confusion and took the phone. He went to close the door, but Danielle crossed her arms.

"This is Mitchell," he said. "Is this Mary?"

Danielle could hear the woman's muffled voice. Her words came out in quick bursts, but Danielle couldn't make them out. Mitchell for his part, kept clenching and unclenching his jaw when he listened.

"I did," he nodded, holding the phone closer to his ear. "Are you okay? Are you in trouble?"

Danielle leaned against the doorframe, trying to get close enough to hear what the woman said in response. But she still couldn't make it out.

"I'm not sure what I can do from the house. It's getting kind of late," Mitchell said into the phone. He turned to Danielle, but quickly darted his eyes away, unable to meet her gaze. He'd been doing that lately, she noticed, unable to make eye contact with her.

Danielle heard the woman mumble something urgently.

Mitchell sighed. "I'm not sure I can get there in time. Can it wait until tomorrow?"

Danielle heard the beep of the line going dead, but Mitchell kept up the charade. "Okay, then, I'll see what I can do." He went so far as to pretend to push the button, and handed the receiver back to Danielle.

"Some kind of emergency?," Danielle asked, not bothering to hide her suspicion.

"Yes," Mitchell nodded. He opened the door to his office just wide enough to squeeze through and closed the door behind him. Danielle heard the lock click behind him.

"I have to go," he said. "There's a thing I have to take

care of at work. Client's had a car accident, they need me on the scene."

She studied him, trying to get a read on what was really going on.

"I see," she said.

He kissed her cheek and headed for the door. He snatched a jacket off of the coat rack, and fumbled pulling the car keys off the rack. "Be back as soon as I can. I promise."

"Okay," she said, and watched him as he quickly made his way into the car.

A few moments later, Danielle watched as Mitchell sped away, pulling out of the driveway recklessly. She picked up the phone and star-sixty-nine'ed the number only to get an error. Whatever number had called her did not exist. Certainly not his office. Certainly not 'Mary From the Office's' cell number.

She was suddenly aware of the small figure at her side, as Allie rubbed her eyes with one hand, and held her rabbit by the ears with the other. She pressed her nose against the window and pointed to the car speeding away.

"Where's Daddy going?" Allie asked, raising her stuffed animal so Mr. Rabbity could see out the window, too.

"Wish I knew, Bunny-bun," she admitted. "But I intend to ask him when he gets back."

— 4.6 —

Gemini had been the one who had left him the document in the diner. The one who had messaged him about his video. When he answered the phone from Mary, she'd sounded like she was in trouble. She told him repeatedly that 'they' had been watching her. They had been following her. That she and he needed a safe place to meet. He was exactly where she had told him to be, on the corner of two filthy streets standing in front of a pay phone, waiting for it to ring.

He'd done everything that Gemini had said. Now, Mitchell was here, alone, pacing by a pay phone covered in cracks and graffiti. The neighborhood itself didn't look all that safe, and he didn't want to stay here any longer than he needed to. The only other car on the street other than his was a rusted heap. A shanty town of worn tents that filled an empty lot surrounded by rusted chainlink was within sight of him. Every few moments, he caught one of the homeless staring at him.

He checked his watch then turned his attention back to the pay phone. His hand repeatedly clenched and unclenched, as he tried to exercise the nervous energy that had built inside him. It was almost exactly two hours since Gemini had hung up on him at his house.

When it finally rang, just as Gemini had promised, Mitchell jumped at it, snatching the receiver off the hook. He'd been practicing what he was going to say. What he wanted to ask. He needed to know what she knew. He needed to know what he'd seen.

Before he could speak, Gemini demanded, "Are you alone? Were you followed?"

Mitchell gathered his strength. "You're going to tell me who you are, right now," he said. "You're going to tell me, or so help me, I'm going to hang up and I am done with you. Do you hear me? I am done."

Gemini asked again — no, she demanded — "Were you followed?"

"No," he said. The entire drive to this corner payphone he'd watched the rearview for any sedans that might be following him.

"Are you sure?" Gemini said. "You have to be sure."

Mitchell spun around, taken aback. And suddenly less certain. What if they had been in another type of car? What if he had been? "I don't know," he admitted, feeling a sudden wave of paranoia.

Gemini pushed. "Think, Mitchell. It's important."

His mind raced, trying to remember the drive. He stammered, "I-I don't think so."

"What about your phone?" Gemini asked. "I tried to reach you there."

"It's been off for days," he said with more confidence. "I was worried they could have hacked it. Listening to me." His eyes moved around the area, making sure there wasn't some federal agent hiding among the homeless.

"Smart, smart. I wish I'd thought of that. I guess it'll have to do," Gemini breathed deeply, letting out a long sigh of relief. "There's a bar three blocks north. Called the Rosewater. Go there. If you see anything suspicious, run.

Don't look back. Just run. You run, do you hear me? Promise me you'll run."

"How will I know you?" he asked.

"Promise me," she said just before the line went dead with a click.

Mitchell listened to the dial tone, and stared at the phone, wondering what to do next.

— 4.7 —

Except for a few barflies scattered at various stools, the Rosewater was empty. Howell sat on one of them, wearing sunglasses, a grey hoodie, a long wig and a fake mustache that was convincing enough provided that no one scrutinized it too much. He watched as every person entered the bar. In the last hour, Athena saw that he barely made a dent in the beer in front of him. Every few minutes he had to assure the bartender that he was fine, and didn't need anything else. Twice, the bartender had tried to strike up a conversation. And, twice, Howell had shot him down. He didn't need another drink. He didn't want to unload his troubles. He wasn't waiting for someone, though this was a lie.

Athena sat in a booth with her back against the wall and stared down at the glass in her hand. It was just ginger ale, but she longed for something stronger. It was all right in front of her. With a wave of her hand she could have the bartender bring her anything she could desire. But, she knew how far down that slippery slope would lead her. With one drink, she'd undo seven years of hard work and discipline. The sins of her past would ride back on a wave of whiskey.

She made an effort not to acknowledge Howell, just as he was trying hard to not make eye contact with her. Every so often she would fail. Every time the door opened, they both perked up, and she hoped no one would pick up on that. When that happened, the bell over the door would ring, and, Athena put on the airs of someone afraid, tense. She'd decided her Gemini persona was someone who was in over her head. Who stumbled upon something she didn't understand. Someone who was through the looking glass and couldn't find her way home.

Very likely, she would have to have to throw this all out the window depending on where Mitchell went with the conversation. As much as she was able to, she had done her homework. She'd done enough live theater to know that sometimes things could just go sideways without warning.

Athena had pieced together a mental image of what he would be like. His writing was haphazard, and composed of run-on sentences. The man clearly was unfamiliar with the proper use of a comma. Mitchell was not prone to quips or engaging in conversations. He did not post memes or emojis in response. There were no public videos of him. Unlike some of the others in the chat room, he didn't have much of an online presence to study.

She'd only ever heard his voice in their brief phone

conversation. But, as Athena had discerned that his wife, Danielle, was listening, she didn't think that it was a good yardstick by which to measure his personality.

She closed her hands on her drink, purposefully trying to make her body language read as guarded and nervous. Finding her, she hoped, would be easy for Vincent, as she was the only woman there.

After three false starts, their target finally stepped into the Rosewater. Mitchell Vincent carried himself with a mix of exhaustion and panic. His eyes were more sullen than the last time she had seen him. He was more gaunt than he had been in his last surveillance photo. His eyes scanned the bar until he landed on her sitting in her booth.

He took a deep breath and headed her way with purpose. She tensed herself for him, widening her eyes and holding her breath. Athena hoped she was ready. She'd been preparing for this moment. She'd run it over a thousand times in her head, and now she sat with the man in the flesh in front of her.

Having Howell there was both a blessing and a curse. She felt safer knowing he was nearby, but now, she knew she had an audience for her performance.

"Are you Gemini?" he asked. Athena could tell that he was shaking, and trying to get himself under control.

"Mitchell?" she whispered. When he nodded, she let her shoulders relax, her eyes whipped around the room going from person to person. "Sit down," she offered.

"I wasn't followed," he said, his head scanning around the room, missing Howell sipping his beer to further obscure his face. Mitchell slid into the booth and leaned in, matching her whisper. "I'm sure of it."

"Good. We can't be too careful," she said, "but, I'm glad you're safe."

"Are you?" Concern crossed his face. "Are you safe?"

"I don't know," she backed away, pressing herself deeper into the booth. She fidgeted with her drink straw.

"Who are you?" he asked.

She'd expected this question and knew how to play it. Athena shook her head. "Best you not know my real name," she said. "Who I am isn't important. I wanted you to know that you're not alone in this. I hope I didn't scare you."

"You didn't," he assured her. Athena couldn't tell if he was lying. His body language was that of a man who was barely maintaining a front of bravery. "That document you gave me, where did it come from?"

Athena leaned in closer. "My husband worked for Glowaski International. I found it in his desk, when I was cleaning it out."

Vincent didn't take the bait about her husband. Maybe she was being too subtle. She'd have to hit that harder. Instead, he pulled out a small notebook, and pulled out a folded piece of paper. She recognized it as the document she left for him, now littered with notes in different colored ink.

"I think I know what part of it is," he said. Mitchell unfolded the memo. "This word here, the one redacted." He spun the page around so that she could read it, and pointed to one of the blacked out bits of information.

"I think it has to be a place," he said. "They didn't quite

do a good job of blacking it out. First letter could be an 'M.' From the date of the memo, this could be related to a UFO crash in Montana six years ago. Weird stuff goes down in Montana; has for years. Lights in the sky. Livestock turned inside out. Rumor is there's a secret military base that's a joint operation between the U.S. and Canadian government. I've searched everywhere for any kind of reference to Project: Carolina, but I can't find anything."

"What could it be?" Athena ran through the permutations of the conversation she had anticipated. Montana was not among them. She had to buy some time while she figured out where to lead him.

"There are a couple of theories floating around on the forums." Mitchell got excited, raising his voice, only to lower quickly again to a whisper. "Some think it's a meaningless code word. Some think it has something to do with the USOs."

Another thread she hadn't expected. "USOs?" she asked, unable to follow his logic. "Like, shows for the military?"

"They're Unidentified Submersible Objects," Mitchell corrected. "Underwater alien sightings."

Athena was taken aback, and was genuinely curious. She'd never heard of underwater starships outside of movies. "Is that a real thing?"

"Some think so." Mitchell flipped through his notebook. Athena saw that it was crammed with his jagged handwriting. There were no lines in the journal, and the further Mitchell flipped through the more irregular the lines of his notes became. "There are sightings all over the world. Off the coast of Japan, and there have been several sightings off Catalina Island in California. But, I don't think that works with the Montana connection to the Carolina codeword."

Then inspiration hit her. "He did go to Montana," she added quickly, 'yes-anding' Mitchell's thought. Athena tried to keep her own excitement at the thrill of improv in check. "He said he had an uncle there. A park ranger or something, but I never met him. He never even referred to him by anything other than his initials. J.L." She made mental note about putting some thought into 'Uncle J.L.' as a potential lead for later.

Mitchell thought for a moment. "I wonder if that means anything?"

Again, Mitchell didn't take the thread about her missing husband. It was time to redirect the conversation.

"This 'Project: Carolina,'" she said, "What do you think it is?" She'd designed it to be an open clue, as Franklin had suggested. And turning back to her theater youth, eagerly awaited to play off whatever Mitchell could come up with.

Mitchell pursed his lips. He took the document back and folded it carefully. He closed his notebook. "The most interesting theory has been this. Someone has suggested that it might have something to do with a new kind of technology. Something big. South Carolina was 'first in flight' after all. Maybe it's something like that. We need more information."

First in flight, she thought. *I can absolutely use that.* She smiled despite herself, and quickly shut it down. She needed to remain in character.

"What?" Mitchell asked. She didn't think Mitchell noticed the smile, but she was wrong.

Athena straightened, wiping any hint of expression off of her face. It was time to throw some more fuel on the fire.

"It's just," she began, and reached into her bag underneath the table, "I found other papers, too. I don't know what they mean. But I was hoping you might be able to make sense of them." She pulled out a manilla file folder, and feigned looking around nervously, as she opened it to reveal a stack of documents like the one that she had left him in the diner.

Mitchell's eyes went wide when he saw the handful of redacted pages, wrinkled from shoving them into her filing cabinet and smashing them a few times to make them appear worn.

"I was afraid to upload them myself," she said. Athena slid the file folder across the table to him. "Do these mean anything to you?"

Mitchell flipped through the pages, his eyes racing over them. "This!" he said louder than he'd probably intended.

Out of the corner of her eye, she caught Howell straightening. Mitchell picked up one of the pages and turned around to face Athena. He tapped a set of numbers he found in the middle of a paragraph.

Just as she'd hoped.

"These numbers are a set of coordinates," he continued, correcting his level of volume. "Longitude and latitude." He held another of them to the light above their booth. "This could be some kind of schematic. Part of a patent application, maybe?"

Then, Mitchell paused, with concern in his tired eyes. He swallowed and said, "What happened to your husband?"

Finally, she thought. She should have expected this. Mitchell's writings often jumped from one thought to another. His thoughts were often non-linear.

Athena turned away, trying to calculate the right amount of pause she needed to convey both hesitancy and uncertainty. She lowered her head and frowned.

"I wish I could tell you," she said. She averted her gaze, and thought of her own husband, and how badly that had gone. Draw on your own experience, her acting coach had taught her. And the fresh pain of waking up to an empty bed with Howard having left in the middle of the night washed over her.

When she looked back up to meet Mitchell's gaze, she caught herself on the edge of genuine tears. She wiped her eyes and tried to hold them back. The tears continued to well, and she struggled to keep herself in the moment.

"I wish I knew," she managed, with a convincing quiver in her voice.

Mitchell closed the folder. His hands fidgeted, and his jaw clenched. "He's gone isn't he?"

"He disappeared three years ago," she said, wiping away the tear. *Keep the story thread open,* she reminded herself, *let his imagination run wild.* And if his posts and this encounter were any indication, Athena figured Mitchell's imagination would do just that.

"I'm so sorry." Mitchell reached for her hand, catching her by surprise.

Instinctively she jerked her hand away, and leaned back in the booth. Out of the corner of her eye, she saw Howell stiffen and heard the clink of him setting his beer on the bar. She knew the signal. If she said, 'umbrella,' he would come running. But it was not time for that yet.

Mitchell pulled his own hands back. Her reaction triggered something in him, embarrassment? Pity?

"Three years after the crash in Montana," Mitchell said. "Did you know what he was working on at — where was it?"

"Glowaski International," she said, knowing the gibberish URL hidden in the documents she'd handed him would lead him to the directory she'd planted there. "And he never told me what he was working on. He wasn't allowed to. He never even hinted, but that always made me worry. I was always afraid he was working on something terrible; weapons."

Mitchell put his hand on the documents folder. "What do you know about them?" Mitchell asked.

Then, inspiration hit her. A potential connection to 'Uncle J.L.' and Jet Propulsion Labs in Pasadena. She wondered if Mitchell would follow the breadcrumbs.

"They develop new technologies, clean energy research, and weapons for the military," she said, starting what she knew to be true about them. Then, she began to spin the narrative. "I know they did some consulting for JPL and NASA. Howard was an engineer. He went to Pasadena to meet with JPL a few times. That's all I know." She'd purposefully used Howard's name to make her pain appear more real to Mitchell.

Because it was.

It must have worked. Mitchell leaned in and said just above a whisper. "I'm going to find out the truth, Gem. I promise you, I'll find out what's going on."

This time, it was her that took his hand. Across the bar, she caught Howell tensing again. Below the table, she waved Howell down with her other hand. The man continued to sit on his stool pretending to sip his beer, but never took his eyes off of her. She forced a smile.

"Whatever you do, be careful, Mitchell. Please, for the sake of yourself and your family, be careful." She patted the file folder. "Take those," she said. "I'm going dark for a while. If I find anything else, I'll be in touch."

Mitchell picked up the folder and gripped it tight. He picked up his notebook, and rose from the table.

"I have to go. But, be safe," he said. "You never know who's watching. I want you to know, you're not alone, either. We're in this together. We'll expose them for what they've done. We'll find the truth, no matter where it leads."

"Thank you," she said, and watched him go.

After Mitchell stepped out of the door, Athena allowed herself to make eye-contact with Howell. Her audience of one raised his glass of beer in salute. They had arrived separately, and the plan was for them to leave separately. She waited until her heart rate lowered enough before she got up, left a twenty on the table, and left the Rosewater behind.

A smile broke over her face as she thought of the mountain of work ahead.

That couldn't have gone better.

CHAPTER FIVE

LYING FOR THE TRUTH

— 5.1 —

"Gerry, I don't expect you to take what I say at face value," Cavanaugh said not just to him, but to the entire ballroom audience facing them. "I expect you to do your research. I expect you to challenge your own assumptions. To examine the evidence, and when the evidence doesn't add up, to add it again until it does."

She was getting under his skin, and it showed on Gerry Henry's face. "And I suppose," he said through clenched teeth, "that you have more fabricated facts to back up your argument that ancient man wasn't influenced by otherworldly powers?"

"Fabricated?" she asked, incredulously.

"You need something to back up what you're saying," he said. "We've seen again and again, example after example of extraterrestrial influence, and you've refused to accept any of it."

"I have to say that burden of proof is on the one making the irrational claim," she said. "Not on the one making the reasonable one."

"Irrational," Henry growled.

"But, facts don't matter to you, apparently," she said. "How many times do these theories need to be debunked before you accept what's right in front of you? Harry Houdini debunked countless mediums countless times in a countless different ways and it did nothing, absolutely nothing, to dissuade anyone who was a true believer from the notion that psychic powers exist."

"They do, of course," a voice came from further down the dais. Abraham Stanislav leaned forward.

"That's certainly one way to look at it," Cavanaugh snapped. She saw Stanislav, fidgeting with his water bottle, swinging it in an almost mesmerizing rhythm. Perhaps he was tired of seeing his friend Henry get redder and redder as Cavanaugh countered him on point after point. From what she could tell, Henry wasn't used to having his work as a paranormal and extraterrestrial expert challenged. She wasn't as familiar with Stanislav's work, but she knew a fraud when she saw one.

Cavanaugh was smelling blood in the water, and just as she was moving in for the kill, Stanislav decided he wanted to go a few rounds.

"I don't need facts," he cooed with his smooth voice. "I have faith. Faith in a world beyond what we can see and touch. A world that is mysterious and magical beyond what we experience in our normal lives."

"What?" Cavanaugh stifled a laugh. "Are you serious?"

"I'm not the only one." Stanislav gestured to the crowd and they returned the gesture with a round of applause.

Cavanaugh felt her heart sink.

— 5.2 —

Mitchell was trying to make as little noise as possible when he opened the door. He'd pulled his shoulder bag off, eager to get into his office to examine the things that Gemini had given him. He'd only been able to get a glance at their contents at the Rosewater, and it was an extreme act of will to keep from pulling over to the side of the road and poring over them.

He needed to get them scanned. He needed to get them to the community as quickly as possible. He needed to get more minds on it. If Gemini was in danger because of what her husband had done, and if he could help, he would. Maybe he could get the Strange Sightings community to connect the dots between what he had seen and Gemini's husband's disappearance.

Crossing the room to head to his office, Mitchell was deep in thought as a lamp snapped on, startling him. The light revealed Danielle, arms folded, sitting in the lounge chair, and glaring at him.

"How was work?" she asked, cooly.

Mitchell slowly pulled his jacket off and hung it on the coat rack. "You didn't have to wait up," he said, trying to hide his surprise. "You should be in bed."

"I'm not," Danielle said. He knew her expression of quiet rage well. He'd rarely seen her that furious before. She rose from the chair moving slowly as if she'd been sitting there a long time. "How's Mary?"

"Who?" The word was out of Mitchell's mouth before he could stop it.

"*Who?*" Danielle repeated through clenched teeth. "The woman on the phone. Who was she?"

Mitchell hesitated, and clutched his bag tightly. "She's no one," he said. "I swear."

"Bullshit," Danielle spat.

Mitchell knew he couldn't tell the truth. Not yet. He knew that Danielle would never believe him until he had answers. He would need some kind of concrete proof. He just had pieces of information. The spider's web was coming together, but it wasn't there yet. He had to figure out how to hold her off, at least, util he knew more.

"Nothing," he said, trying to choke down the feeling of violation of her going through his computer. "Nothing's going on."

"Don't lie to me," she warned. "What's happening,

Mitchell? Who is this Mary? She's not from your work, that's for damned sure."

Mitchell's hands clenched his satchel. He didn't know what to say, so he made the mistake of saying nothing.

"You think I'm stupid?" she asked, stepping closer. Her eyes were quivering in rage. "You think I don't know that you've been getting up in the middle of the night? Where do you go?"

"Danielle," he tried to assure her, "it's not an affair."

"Then what is it?" He saw her jaw move under her cheek as she ground her teeth. "It's that damned video, isn't it?"

Mitchell broke her gaze, and took a step back.

"I went into your office. I went through your browser history."

"You went into my office?" he shouted, feeling suddenly ashamed and betrayed.

"Don't wake Allie," she said. "And don't raise your voice to me."

He couldn't remember if he'd used a private browser. Couldn't remember the last time he cleared his history. He'd been using a VPN to mask his true identity online, but never imagined that his own wife would invade his privacy like that. What had she seen? Had she read the forums? His notes?

She must have read his expression, or caught him touching his scar — she knew this to be the obsessive-compulsive tell he did when he was anxious — because Danielle turned away from him. "You said you'd stop,

Mitchell. You promised you'd stop."

"I know," he whimpered.

"You promised!" she shouted.

Mitchell started to feel his own anger rising in him mixed with shame and confusion. His thoughts twisted inside of him, and he was unsure what was going to come out. He could feel himself about to spin out of control.

He centered himself. Forced himself to calm down. He took a deep breath and counted to three. Then, he said, "I know, I promised."

"Then keep it," she growled. "I'd almost wished you were having an affair. That'd be normal, at least! What's this?" She knelt down to reach for a piece of paper that must have fallen out of his jacket.

She picked up the piece of paper and held it up to him. It was the copied document Gemini had left for him at the Starlight.

"What is this?" she demanded, her expression a mixture of confusion and anger. "Is this part of it?"

He took the paper in his shaking hands. "It's nothing," he said.

"Then tear it up," she said.

He felt the paper in his hands, and in that moment of hesitation, Danielle stormed out of the room swearing under her breath.

Mitchell wondered what to do, and followed her into the bedroom. He finally caught up to her, as she lay on the bed turned away from him.

Mitchell stood in the doorway, with Gemini's original

document in his hands. "I'm sorry," he said. "I'm so sorry, Danny."

Danielle was crying. "Tell me it's over."

He leaned down and kissed the back of her neck, but instead of easing, she tensed. She pulled away for a second, then leaned into him resting her head on his chest.

"It's over," he said. "I swear." Mitchell took the Starlight document in his hand and showed it to her. He slowly, deliberately, ripped it in half and let the pieces fall to the floor.

Danielle relaxed, but her face was still twisted in worry. "I hope so," she said.

She rolled in bed, and he put his arm around her.

After a long silence, she added, "I love you."

"I love you, too," he said, but the words were little more than an automated response.

His mind was elsewhere. Several elsewheres, actually. All he could think about were the pages that Gemini had given him. He had to get to his notebook and start to piece the puzzle together. He was counting the seconds until she was asleep and he could take a closer look at the pages in his satchel.

Part of him knew the truth. Mitchell wasn't sure he would be able to stop. He knew that somewhere in those papers must be the answer to the Carolina mystery. Its connection to Montana. To Gemini and Glowaski International. To the truth. He had to find it.

If Danielle was going to go into his office while he wasn't there, he would have to be more careful about his computer use in the future. He might have to get a new lock on the door, one where she wouldn't have a key.

He thought of the torn pieces of the document from the Starlight and felt comforted in the fact that he could always print another.

— 5.3 —

"There's a lot of talk on the forums," Athena said as the presentation slide behind her advanced to a screenshot of the sub-forum that Mitchell Vincent used most frequently, "that this might be the 'first' of something." She tapped her laptop and the screenshot of the discussion thread changed to show a few key phrases highlighted. She indicated a section of the conversation with a laser pointer.

"Interesting," Franklin said from the darkness of the Area Fifty-One conference room. With the lights dimmed, Athena could barely make out the Director and a handful of other Agents in the project update. Over the last few weeks, her team had grown from just her and a few freelancers to on-site designers, to two analysts who monitored the internet chatter and compiled briefings and spotted trends in the conversations, and Howell, who had now been assigned to her full time. She also had a software developer overseeing any technical aspects of the project, including getting the files she'd created onto the Glowaski server. She thought his name was actually Robert, but everyone called him Bugs.

"I like that," she said, circling the word 'first' on the screen with her laser pointer before showing digital versions of the documents that she had dumped on Mitchell's lap at the Rosewater. "I think that's very interesting and I intend to follow that narrative trajectory. There are two bits of information on the documents I gave to Vincent that should lead them to a server on the Glowaski International data base. The page is awaiting a password, which they should be able to group-think to find an answer."

She changed slides again to another discussion thread. "They're already talking about it," she said. "Once they crack the password, we can drive them to this."

She revealed a photo of a sheet of metal carved with alien runes and circle patterns.

"This was done by our friend in Osaka," she said. "That's where our alien hieroglyphs and star charts come in. They're loosely based on Sumerian writing, so if he wants to make that Chariot-of-the-Gods connection, he can. We've laser-etched them onto paper-thin metal sheets and are dropping some hints in the image's metadata that they're made of an alloy made of metals that are unknown to the periodic chart."

She pointed to a section of the image in the corner. "We purposefully made this section out of focus, so, if we need to, we can add to the narrative later with a better version of this photo. These files are going to be marked classified and encrypted. The encryption will be tough, but hackable."

"How do you know they'll be smart enough to crack

it?" Franklin asked.

"We're dealing with a very driven community here." It was Bugs who piped up and answered. He had shaggy hair and the posture of a man who spent most of his life hunched over a keyboard. "Together, they're smarter and more resourceful than any of us."

Bugs had been leading the charge for any programming efforts that she had needed. He'd been invaluable as she developed the content. He was young, eager, and, like all of them, just a little odd.

Athena nodded. "Only one of them has to be able to solve it, then they all know what's going on. I promise you, we'd never be able to devise a puzzle too hard for this group to solve."

"We designed the page to delete itself after it has been accessed four times," Bugs said, with a hint of pride. "It'll be like the hole in security has been discovered and then sealed. And being on an official Glowaski server will definitely add legitimacy."

"Why are you making them jump through all these hoops?" another Agent, Jasper Lee of the 'Fidget' project, asked. He ran a social media meme generator designed to promote radical alien theories. Mostly, she had deduced, Lee sat in his office and thought of alien-related puns. As much as this was a briefing for Franklin, it was a peer review as well. "Couldn't we just do another info dump on Mr. Vincent if we need to?"

Franklin raised a finger. "It's important that they find as much as possible themselves," he said. "Simms has already dropped too much on Vincent personally." There was a hint of scolding in his words. She knew he hadn't approved of her being so in the weeds, but she moved on.

"I don't want to be the one only leaving all the breadcrumbs," she said, "or Mitchell might become suspicious. If we need to, we'll use another of the dummy accounts on the forums to push them in the right direction. Bugs has been running *Final_Forumteer* from time-to-time and Lacy has been monitoring the bot accounts of *Saucerman* and *Klaatu_51*."

"Why 'Carolina?'" Lee asked.

"Why not? A completely random choice on my part," she shrugged. "I planted a few loose threads to give them enough latitude to make their own story."

"Like a dungeon master?" Bugs asked.

Howell let out a derisive snort.

"Actually, yes," Athena said. "It's a great deal like that. Create a broad world and let the players — in this case, the community — help define it. Focus in on the direction you think they're going and flesh that out. Anticipate what they're going to do and what they're going to find." Then, she winked at Howell. "And don't mock. Dungeons and Dragons is fun."

Franklin snapped his finger. A wide smile was spread across his face. "Love it."

"What are they going to find at the end of this maze?" Agent Dunham of Operation: Bluewater asked. Despite her weeks at the agency, Athena still wasn't sure what Bluewater was, though she guessed it had something to do with the moon. She had to admit, Dunham ran a tight ship.

"If they follow the breadcrumbs, why, the truth about Carolina, of course." Athena went to the next slide in her presentation, to reveal a schematic of an engine. "That NASA and Glowaski International have been working on a secret engine prototype, one reverse-engineered from an alien craft that crashed in the mountains of Montana six years ago. A faster-than-light interstellar drive — the first of its kind — Codenamed: Kitty Hawk."

"Hence, 'Carolina,'" Franklin clapped his hands in glee. "That, ladies and gentlemen, is how it's done." Franklin signaled to the back of the conference room, and Howell raised the lights. Franklin opened his arms to the rest of the briefing room. "To think she's done all this with a little manpower, a few phone calls, a few websites and a few scraps of paper."

Athena took a bow, but, outside the conference room, the shadows of agents raced past in a panicked hurry. Everyone in the Area Fifty-One conference room tensed.

"What's going on?" she asked.

Franklin rose as his phone buzzed. He opened the door. "Report!" he ordered.

A woman in a gray pantsuit and slicked-back black hair stopped and turned to him. Athena thought she was assigned to Bluewater.

"The Prototype has gone down," the woman said. "Malfunction in the controls. Pilot was able to eject in time. The base is scrambling to get a crew to clean up the wreckage before anyone else can get to it."

Everyone in the conference room sprang into action, then, Athena's eyes went wide as inspiration hit her like a refreshing wave of cool water.

"No! Wait!" she called. The possibilities started to form in her mind as everyone turned towards her.

"We can use this," she said.

"How?" Agent Howell asked.

The words came out slowly, but, as they did they grew in confidence as Athena's plan formed. "We show him — Vincent — the crash site, give him a good look, up close. Then, feed him the bit about the weird metal. Tell him he's been right all along, aliens are behind everything."

Franklin mulled it. "Risky."

"It'll be the proof he's been begging for," she said. "It'll really put this thing over the top. You said you wanted this to be a new Roswell. We can make that happen. Mitchell can be our Farmer Brazel. Hell, we'll make him famous."

She saw the trepidation in Franklin, but she decided to push. "Your pilot is safe, and we might not get another opportunity to do this. Just give me time before they send in your crew. That's all I ask, boss," she said, then added with glee, "We can use this!"

Howell turned to Franklin. "Boss?"

"You have twelve hours," Franklin nodded to Athena. "Do it. I have to make some calls."

Athena let out a squeal of delight and got to work. She had a lot to do on the flight back to Arizona.

— 5.4 —

Danielle listened to the phone ring, uncertain if she should answer. She held the receiver in her hand, feeling its vibration every time it rang. The bright green screen on the receiver read simply, Unknown Caller. Every ring gave Danielle Vincent an increased sense of dread.

It had been three days since Mitchell had renewed his promise to drop his obsession, but since then, he'd been sullen, withdrawn. As she had pressed to find out what was wrong, he'd said he was merely tired. But, simply trying to hang out with him after Allie had gone to bed, he'd stare blankly at the television, sitting next to her. It was almost as if he were waiting for the night to end so he could go back to sleep.

Except he wasn't sleeping. Two of the last three nights, she'd rolled over to find him gone again. The first time, she found him in the dining room, making notes on some paperwork 'from work,' he'd said. The second time, she'd found him in his office staring at the screen. He'd even gone through the pretext of turning his monitor around to show her he'd just been reading the news.

Insomnia had been a side effect of one of his medications in the past, but she was pretty certain he hadn't taken them in the last week at least. He'd been edgy, filled to the brim with nervousness. He'd been tapping his leg, chewing his fingernails, drumming his fingers, and rubbing his scar practically non-stop for days.

On the seventh ring, she finally answered the phone.

Before she could say anything, a woman's voice

practically exploded in her ear. "Is Mitchell there? It's urgent!"

Danielle recognized 'Mary's' voice instantly. Her hand gripped the receiver rightly. "One sec," she said. She took a deep breath, counted to ten, then, in a deeper voice added, "Hello?"

"Mitchell," the woman said, "something's happened. I know it's dangerous, but, you have to meet me at the Starlight as soon as you can. Bring your camera, phone, whatever. Hurry."

The line went dead, and Danielle stared at the receiver. Danielle hit the call back button only to hear a familiar ring of beeps and an automated voice respond, "I'm sorry. The number you have dialed has been disconnected or is no longer in service. Please hang up and try your number again."

"Of course," she said. Danielle had expected nothing else.

She hung up the phone with a beep, and set it on the dining room table.

"Mitchell, honey?" she called. "I have to run to the store. Can you watch Allie?"

Through the closed door of his office, he called back. "Uh, okay."

She heard the rustle as he got up and opened the door. At least, she noted, it hadn't been locked.

"Is everything okay?" he asked. She thought he looked exhausted, and sweaty.

"Yeah, nothing important," she lied, turning towards

the door. "Back in two."

Danielle managed to keep her poise as she grabbed her jacket and the car keys. Though, she slammed the door to the house harder than she'd intended.

Once in the car, she opened her phone and did a search for 'Starlight' on the map. The only thing that came up in the area was a small diner near the military base, twenty-one minutes away by the phone's estimation. She hit the button for directions and grabbed the steering wheel.

She was a ball of rage when she put the car in drive, and peeled out into the night. In the twenty-one minutes it took her to get to the parking lot, she let out a litany of swears, unsure what she would do. She absently followed the instructions from the voice of her phone until she pulled into the sparsely-populated parking lot, barely aware of the trip she had just made.

From the car, she could see a few people through the window. Her eyes went to the brown-haired woman sitting at the end of the diner. Danielle gritted her teeth and jerked the car door open.

The door swung open with the bright ring of a bell, and her eyes went from person-to-person. A beefy trucker at the counter, wearing a blue mesh-back hat. The lone waitress, Penny from her name tag, leaned over flirting with him. A large man in a white hat looming over the grill. A middle-aged couple having burgers. In the far corner, the brown-haired mouse of a woman sipped from a white coffee cup. She was small, slightly overweight with her hair pulled back into a pony tail. Black glasses that were too big for her rested on her face. Behind them, the woman's unremarkable brown eyes went wide when she saw Danielle barreling towards her.

"Who the fiery hell are you?" Danielle demanded as every head in the diner turned towards her.

Danielle knew that she'd been recognized. She stormed over to the woman, who swore under her breath.

"Hey, Lady, you can't — " Penny the Waitress began, but fell quickly silent when she locked eyes with Danielle. The trucker at the bar turned with open concern on his face.

"Zip it," she snapped, then she turned back to the brown-haired woman. "I asked you a question."

"I'm nobody," the woman said.

"I mean," she growled, "who the fuck are you to my husband? Why are you talking to him? Why are you calling my husband in the dead of night?"

The woman hesitated.

"Don't you fuck with me," Danielle said and slapped the table, rattling the silverware. "You know who I am. I want to know who the fuck are you to my husband?"

She held her coffee in both hands. She stared into it.

"You fucking look at me," Danielle said. The woman did as she was told. Danielle could see her wheels turning, and wondered what lies she was concocting. "If you're going to drag Mitchell into the dark, you're sure as hell are going look me in the eye."

"I'm helping him," she said finally.

"Bullshit."

"No, Danielle. I'm —" the woman began, but this time

Danielle banged the table with all her might. The coffee overturned, and the woman inched further and further back into her booth.

"Hey!" Penny the Waitress shouted. "I'm going to have to ask you to leave!" The trucker got out of his seat, and Danielle could swear he was staring right at the brown-haired woman in the booth.

Danielle ignored Penny the Waitress. "Who are you to say my name? You're part of this, aren't you? Are you part of this alien shit?"

The woman lowered her gaze. "I don't know what to say."

"Don't look away from me," Danielle challenged. "Are you part of this?"

The woman remained silent. Whoever she was, Danielle could tell she was out of her depth and wasn't ready for this conversation.

"Ma'am," the trucker said. "You need to remain calm."

"This doesn't concern you, sir," Danielle told the man, never taking her eyes off the woman in the booth. "Answer me, goddamn it! Are you involved in this shit?"

"I am," she said, weakly.

Danielle crossed her arms. "Do you have any idea what you're doing to him?"

At her words, Danielle saw the shock cross the woman's face. The shock was followed quickly by doubt and shame. Danielle knew she had no idea. Or the thought had never occurred to her.

"I thought not," Danielle said.

"Is he," she stammered, "is he okay?"

"Not even close," Danielle shook her head in disgust. She shoved a finger in the woman's face. "You stay the hell away from my husband. You stay the hell away from my family. If you ever call my house, talk to Mitchell, or if I ever see you again, god help you."

Danielle picked up the coffee cup, and poured whatever had been left in the cup onto the woman's lap just to watch her scramble out of the way. Then, Danielle threw the cup and it shattered against the diner wall, and the woman flinched, rightfully afraid.

"What are you doing?" Penny the Waitress shouted. The man behind grill was also yelling from the back.

Danielle turned to go and brushed past the trucker. She passed the couple staring at her, Penny the Waitress, and shoved the pie rack on the counter. It came crashing to the floor causing a roar of insults from Penny the Waitress and a man from the kitchen.

"Oh, fuck off!" Danielle called, then turned to Penny the Waitress. "Don't worry, hon, she'll pay for those!" She shot the woman in the corner one last, disgusted sneer before throwing the door open with another rattle of the bell.

Danielle stormed back to her car, and left the commotion of the Starlight Diner behind.

— 5.5 —

Her heart felt like an empty hole in her chest and for the first time, Athena Simms questioned exactly what she had done to Mitchell Vincent. When Danielle had asked her if she knew what she was doing to him, she had to admit to herself she didn't.

She could not stop shaking, still rattled from Danielle storming into the diner. Not rattled, scared. Danielle Vincent could have had a gun, or just pulled a dull knife from the table and stabbed her with it. And she wasn't sure that Howell would have been able to get to her in time before either of those things could have happened.

She leaned against the back of Howell's rental in the parking lot of the Starlight Diner. On the way there, he had pulled over to throw clods of dirt and mud at the silver pickup, because he had thought it was too clean. At the time, she'd thought it amusing, now, with the dirt on her hands, it felt less so.

She held her cellphone in her hand with Franklin's private number queued up, not wanting to make the call.

Then, Howell opened the door to the Starlight Diner, still wearing his blue trucker hat. Waving back to Penny the Waitress, he made his way towards Athena. As he moved further away from the diner, his trucker swagger gave way to his more usual rigid, measured steps.

"I left a substantial tip. Everything is under control," Howell said. As he got closer, and he saw her leaning against his truck and shaking, concern crossed his face.

"How I wish that were true," she managed.

"You okay?" he asked.

"I don't think so," she said. Best she tell someone the truth about something, she figured. Athena's thumb hovered over the call button, and she forced herself to press it. A few moments later, Director Franklin answered, demanding an update. His words blurred in her mind.

"Send in your crew, sir. Mitchell's not coming," she said.

Franklin spoke, but she didn't really hear what he was saying. She guessed he was asking why.

"I... I don't know," she said, on autopilot.

Fury built in her until she threw the phone with all her might. The phone landed with a crunch on the gravel parking lot. She hunched over, on the verge of tears.

Athena let out a primal howl of rage, so loud Penny the Waitress, from inside the Starlight, looked up from cleaning the pie avalanche. Howell reached out to help, but he stopped when Athena held out a hand.

"Don't," she tried to say, but she could barely breathe. Barely think. She was barely aware of those in the diner that had her undivided attention, whether she wanted it or not. They were all staring at her.

She let out another scream and she felt herself hyperventilating. Athena tried to will herself calm. She let in deep breaths, and pushed them out slowly. She could fix this. She had to. If she could just push back the rage, and the shock, she could —

Then, it hit her. She could *use* this.

It would be a stop-gap measure for sure, but she could make it work. She had to. She crossed the parking lot and picked up her phone with the now cracked screen.

She could hear Franklin's faint voice. "Simms?" Franklin asked. "Are you there? Simms, please respond."

"Here's what we do," she said, her voice shaking. "Have the team take lots of photos. Get as much coverage as we can. I'll review the photos as soon as I get them. We'll have our guy in Osaka doctor them sloppily to make it appear like we're covering up something. We'll set it up as part of a Phase Three of the information dump. I'll be on location within the hour. Then, we'll regroup tomorrow and I'll present our next steps."

"Acknowledged, Simms," Franklin said. "You sound a little out of sorts. What happened with Mitchell?"

"He didn't show," she said, knowing a lie of omission was still a lie. She'd have to figure out how to spin Danielle's appearance to Franklin, but that was a problem for another day.

"This isn't an exact science, sometimes things don't go our way," he said. "As long as you're okay."

"Yes," she lied. "I'll report more as soon as I can."

"I look forward to it," Franklin said.

"Thank you, sir." Simms put her phone up as Howell came closer. She wiped the last of her tears from her eye sand turned to him. "Let's go. I need to figure out what to do next."

CHAPTER SIX

THE FACTS ABOUT FAITH

— 6.1 —

Stanislav leaned back, a self-assured smile on his face. "So, let's speak of faith and fact, shall we?" he said. "Very often the two intersect in ways that boggle the imagination. In religious texts around the world, from the Mahabharata to the Bible, we can find references to events that could only be interpreted as extraterrestrial in nature. Strange visitations, alien encounters, technology far beyond the comprehension of ancient man. In the Mahabharata, for example, there are clues that point to starships and nuclear technology. In the Bible, Moses spoke to the burning bush.

Ezekiel saw a flying saucer, describing angels that are
nothing like the imagery we know today, but truly alien in
their appearance. He also described them to have a strange
vehicle, which he called wheels-within-wheels. Does that
not sound like an alien craft?"

Stanislav smirked as if he just dropped a bomb on
Margo Cavanaugh. He opened his palm, welcoming a
response. She was, for her part, not impressed.

"Operative words there are 'could be interpreted,'" she
said. "Ezekiel does refer to angels lifting the throne of god
that has wheels within wheels, but that's a bit of a leap to go
from 'man-describing-bonkers-hallucination' to 'there-are-
aliens-and-this-is-definitive-proof.'"

"Oh, ye of little faith," he said.

Cavanaugh threw up her hands as if to say, of course.
"To suggest that his description of the vehicle in his vision
is some kind of spacecraft," she said, "and that the
cherubim are some kind of aliens is more than a little far-
fetched. That's one hell of an interpretation." Before he
could respond she added, "One hell of an unsubstantiated
interpretation."

"And yet," he said is his smooth, well-rehearsed
performer's rhythm, "there are several examples of Biblical
passages interpreted in Renaissance paintings, and many of
them have what could be interpreted as UFOs." He signaled
to Mad Autumn. "Go to the slide of the *Madonna*, if you
please, my dear."

"Mad Autumn with the *Madonna*," the moderator said,
aiming her clicker. "You got it."

Mad Autumn, Cavanaugh had decided early on in the

panel, was not really helping.

Cavanaugh rolled her eyes when the painting, *Madonna with Child with the Infant St. John,* appeared overhead. It depicted, in addition to the subject of its title, a strange, circular formation in the sky behind Mary with a beam of light streaking from it. This particular section of the painting was highlighted in an insert and blown up. Below this were the image of a man and his dog staring up at the circular object and the ray. She'd seen it before; heard all about the mysterious flying saucer in it. If they were kind enough to lob a softball at her, she was ready to crush it.

"Even the Masters, my dear Ms. Cavanaugh, believed in flying saucers. Those from another world have been visiting us throughout our history," he said. "The evidence is right in front of you, all you have to do is embrace the truth of it all."

"The truth," Cavanaugh sighed. "See that figure there?" she pointed to the man and the dog. "The shepherd and his dog observing the phenomena? They are seen over and over again in other paintings. They're observing a host of angels, which are depicted many times in Renaissance paintings as rings of angels in clouds. This is supposed to be that same ring, only smaller in the sky. And while this example isn't as detailed as others, it, in no way, means there are flying saucers all about shooting lasers at things, or that artists in the Renaissance believed in such things."

— 6.2 —

Mitchell marched Mr. Rabbity towards a giggling Allie, adding a "Boom, boom, boom" with every step.

"Silly!" Allie squealed.

After an impromptu and somewhat messy spaghetti dinner, one of the few things that Mitchell could make with confidence that Allie would actually eat, he'd wiped her face with a towel and thrown Mr. Rabbity into the washing machine after the stuffed animal taken a face dive into the sauce. Mr. Rabbity was now cleaner than he'd been in years and still warm from the dryer.

Activities focused Mitchell, and playing with his daughter gave him a bit of a reprieve from the Glowaski Documents and Carolina. They were looming in the back of his mind though. He was trying to embrace the shower principle, letting something simmer in the far corners of his brain awaiting inspiration, while he did other things.

They had been playing for hours, and he was wondering when Danielle would make her way home before he had to put his daughter to bed. Danielle was gone longer than he'd thought, and directing his attention to Allie kept the dark thoughts at bay.

Did the car break down? Had Danielle been in an accident? Was she hurt? Did he need to call hospitals? Did he —

Mitchell stopped himself from going into a spiral. He knew the thoughts were unrealistic, but that didn't stop them from circling his mind. Instead, he played with Allie, if nothing else, to make up for some of the time he'd spent in his office, rather than with Danielle and her.

He heard the car pull into the driveway. "I bet that's Mommy," he said.

"Yay!" Allie said, snatching Mr. Rabbity from his hand.

Mitchell broke into a smile when the door was thrown open, as if by a raging storm, and Danielle glared at him. Mitchell stopped, his blood running cold.

"Mommy?" she squeaked.

"Hey, honey, did you—?" *find what you were looking for, was what he was going to say,* but he immediately cut himself off when he saw his wife's face. His hands twitched. Whatever had happened to Danielle on her trip, something had gone terribly wrong.

Allie, for her part, pulled the stuffed rabbit close, and her eyes darted from parent to parent, unsure of what was going on. Danielle leaned down to her daughter's level and faked a smile for her.

"Allie, honey, go play in your room," Danielle said in a bright tone. She stroked the girl's hair our of her eyes. "Mommy will be in there to tuck you in in a bit, okay?"

Allie's eyes lowered down at her toy, stroking its ears then up at her mother, uncertain. "Mommy?" she said, but Mitchell understood his daughter's tone. *What's going on?* was what she was really trying to ask.

"Go make up a new story about Mr. Rabbity in the carrot patch," Danielle offered. "I'd love to hear it."

Any worry on the child's face vanished and was replaced with excitement. "I'll draw you a picture!" Allie shouted and bounded out of the room with a burst of speed.

Once Allie was out of the room, Danielle rose and faced him with tears welling in her eyes. "You lied to me," she said with venom. "Again."

"What?" he asked.

"Who is she, Mitchell?"

"Who is who?" Mitchell was beginning to understand who Danielle was talking about, but, how could she?

"The woman on the phone," she snapped, still trying to keep her tone low. "The woman who's been calling you in the dead of night. The woman who was waiting for you at some hole-in-the-wall diner in the middle of nowhere."

Mitchell paused and gauged his wife, unsure if she was ready for the truth. He had no idea how Danielle might know about Gemini.

"I'm close," he said. "I'm so close to what's going on. I can feel it."

"But you can't tell me?"

Mitchell eyed his wife, and decided it was time. It was time to tell her everything, whether she was ready for it or not. "It's bigger than you can imagine," he said, and he caught himself pacing back and forth in the living room. "I'm on to something here. Gemini has been — "

"Who the hell is Gemini?" Danielle interrupted. "Is that her name? Is that who's been calling you?"

"I wasn't the only one who saw the craft in the sky. I was just the one who caught it on video. We've been talking online. She saw it too, Danny. She saw it, too," he said. "I think she's in trouble."

Danielle snorted, "Damn right, she is. This ends now, Mitchell."

Mitchell stopped. "You don't understand. They might kill her."

"Who?" Danielle stepped closer, arms crossed. "Who's going to kill her?"

"These agents, I don't know who they are," he admitted. "They're after her. I saw them, they — that's when this all started. Glowaski International, you see, they make specialized aircraft. I think they reverse-engineered something from a crashed UFO. And this, is all connected."

"You're not making sense." Danielle let out an exasperated sigh. "What are you talking about?"

Mitchell ran back what he'd said in his mind. He needed to slow down. He needed to make her understand. He couldn't tell if she was mad, upset, or confused. Likely, he figured, all three. He decided to start over.

"They might be after me, too," he said.

"What?"

"A few weeks ago," he said, remembering the encounter at the diner. "I left the house and went to the Starlight Diner. I saw these agents chase this woman off. There were two of them in an unmarked police car, I think. She left me a note, Danny," he said. As he spoke, Danielle's eyes widened. "She left me a note, and it's all this redacted stuff. The government, they've built something. Something dangerous. That thing I got on tape. I don't know what it is. But she saw it too. She gave me a copy of this document she got practically covered in black marker. There were barely anything left to read. Whatever it is, it's something codenamed, 'Carolina.'"

"She got it from where?" Danielle asked.

He could tell that Danielle was having trouble getting it. Maybe he was just explaining it wrong. With each question, Mitchell could sense her anger rising, but she had to listen. If he told her everything, she had to listen. If he could just get her to see what he did. If he could just get her to believe.

"Her husband died," he said. "We don't know what happened to him. They were his documents. He worked for a military contractor, Glowaski International. I've seen them on the Glowaski site. I have to find out what's going on."

"No," Danielle said. "You don't. You don't have to do anything. If this woman is in trouble, go to the police."

"And tell them what?" he shouted. "Tell them that the government is after her because she saw a UFO?"

Danielle just stared at him. She swallowed, and said quietly, "Sounds crazy when you say it out loud, doesn't it?"

Mitchell felt his own anger rise. Not just anger, but despair. "Don't do that. Don't dismiss this, Danny. It's not like last time. I swear."

"How?" she said. "How is it not like last time?"

"Last time," he said, "my medication was off. It was making me — "

"Are you even taking them?" Danielle took his hesitation as a 'no.' "Your moods slingshot back and forth. You're not sleeping, you're not eating, I can't tell half the time if you're going to scream, or cry, or," she paused, as if building up the courage what to say next. "Or hurt yourself. I don't know what to do. I don't know how much more I have left in me."

Mitchell felt like he'd been slapped. "Please," he said. "This is serious."

"So am I. I can't take this anymore, Mitchell," she said. "I can't. Why can't you just let it go?"

Mitchell stepped away. He couldn't look at her anymore. His words came out in a mangled blur. "Because that's what they want me to do. Don't you see? They lie to us, and they lie to us, and they lie to us, and we just give up. If I do this, the truth means nothing. We embrace the lie. We keep our heads down and we just let them tell us whatever they want, because we let them."

Danielle took a step back. "How much more of this am I expected to put up with?" she asked. "How much?"

"This is important, Danielle," he said. Mitchell reached for her, but she jerked her hand away.

"So am I," she said. "So is Allie. We're your family."

"If you saw what I saw — "

"I didn't," she snapped. "Even if I did, I can't follow you blindly into this. You know you have a problem, and what do you do? You ignore it and we hope it's going to go away, and pretend everything's okay, but it's not."

Mitchell felt like he was hit in the chest. "That's not fair," he said. "Why are you saying this?"

"You cram it down deep inside and hope it goes away," she said. "You hope you can control it. There are pills you won't take. Therapists you won't see. Help you won't take because you think you can handle this on your own. But you can't. I want to help you, but I don't know how."

Mitchell knew how he could get her to believe. "I have to show you," he said. "Follow me."

"Show me what?" she said, walking after Mitchell as he made his way to his office. He went down the hallway to his office, and opened the door, flipping on his desk lamp.

"Here," he said, he started by handing her the printout of the engines. He spoke slowly, trying to connect the dots between the sighting, the schematics, the redacted memos, and what he'd learned from Gemini. He went through it as thoroughly as he could. He had to keep stopping and starting. As he went through the evidence — he had stacks of documents downloaded from the hacked site, dozens of photos — new ideas came to him, almost faster than he himself could keep up. Books that had been ripped apart and pieced back together. Once she heard it, once he explained it, once he showed her, she had to believe him.

She had to.

He went through the connections between Gemini's missing husband, to the crash in Montana, to the mysterious Kitty Hawk Drive, which a Glowaski memo promised by to revolutionize how humans travel. But, once he finished, the expression on her face said it all.

Danielle didn't understand. Or, Mitchell feared, she refused to understand. If she would just listen. Every point he made, every dot he connected, every piece of the puzzle he showed her, she became sadder and sadder. Mitchell saw the evidence now scattered across his desk. Some of that evidence that was literally in her hands. It was so obvious.

Why couldn't she see it? Why couldn't she believe? It was right in front of her.

Did they get to her? he wondered. *Is that where she went to night? Is that why she wouldn't listen?*

She held a memo from Glowaski in her hands. It looked like a circuit board, or something. Mitchell had explained how it connected his video with the Montana crash, and the Kitty Hawk project.

"I think I see now what I have to do," she said, just above a whisper. She crushed the document in her hand.

"Get out."

— 6.3 —

Athena moved as if through a fog. She'd sat silently during Franklin's morning staff meeting with the other project leads. She barely heard the updates from the others, and just muttered the briefest of reports when it came around to her. Everything was moving according to schedule. They were getting traction in the community forming around the project.

Everything was fine, she had lied. She didn't even really hear Franklin's congratulations.

All she could think about was the fear and hate on Danielle Vincent's face.

They'd permanently taken over the Roswell conference

room as their official war room. And the team had swelled from just her toiling away in her cubicle to six fully-dedicated Agents at her disposal. The walls were lined with four-by-eight-foot blackboard with barely any room left on them. In the project war room, she let Bugs do most of the talking during her own project team meeting. He'd been monitoring the traffic on the Glowaski site. The group — there were now probably dozens of active members all stemming from Mitchell's initial post — had downloaded about sixty-percent of the documents. There had been three new videos posted about Carolina. Most of them were still images of the documents pulled from the forums and talking heads covering the same bits of conjecture. Each one was getting views in the tens of thousands. The comments on them ran the gamut of users posting logical fallacies of the posts, those backing the facts of the posts, and the usual noise of spam and hate.

Word of 'The Kitty Hawk Conspiracy,' as it was being called, was spreading. She'd passed *Geminii_22* to another member of the team, having written six pages of potential responses to questions and information she had guessed was coming. The personality was active on four other sites, including a surprisingly active subreddit devoted to the KHC. The *Geminii_22* persona had evolved to include a Twitter account and was sending out a choreographed conversation between itself and a handful of other bot accounts they were monitoring.

There was even rumors that the incident would be covered in the next season of *Alien Truth*. It was the lead story for the conspiracy newsletter, *The Unknown Journal*.

The podcast of the same name had done an episode on it. The producer had even reached out to Geminii_22 to be on the show through the forums.

The buzzwords she had planted in the documents — Carolina, Arclight, Kitty Hawk — were even being picked up on international intelligence reports. Both the Russians and the Chinese had been following the development. One meme from a Russian meme farm even produced a series of online posts using images from Mitchell's video and variations on a theme — *What Else Isn't Your Government Telling You?*

When Bugs turned to her in the middle of the meeting, she had to shake off the malaise, and wound up snapping at him.

"What?" she asked sharply, but knew Bugs didn't deserve her tone.

"I was just wanting to confirm how this affects the timeline?" he said, pointing to the color-coded beat-list for the information. "We still have all these Glowaski bits to dole out."

She waved away the concern. "I don't think it does," she said, promising to review it in the afternoon. This became her refrain through the rest of the meeting. Later. Soon. Will take it under consideration. Will get back to you on that. Throughout the rest of the meeting, her mood darkened.

I'm just tired, she told to herself. But she knew this was a lie of omission, at best. Yes, she was tired, but the guilt, worry, and fear that crept into her mind was there too.

It wasn't until Howell stood to give his part of the

briefing that she snapped out of her own mind to hear Mitchell's name. She realized that Howell had brought up an image of Mitchell onto the screen. It took her a few moments to hear what he was actually saying.

" — withdrew a substantial amount of cash," Howell was saying, "and hasn't been seen since. He hasn't been home. He hasn't been to work. Hasn't used his telephone, or his credit cards. The last known detail is that his car was found in a grocery store parking lot, abandoned, sixteen days ago."

"He hasn't logged onto the forums in that time, either," Bugs added.

Athena's blood went cold. "Sixteen days?" she echoed. "What about Danielle?"

"Filed a missing persons report with the police," Howell said. "But they've had about as much luck as we have."

"And we have no idea where he is?" she asked. "How is that possible?

Howell shook his head. "Wherever he is, he's off the grid."

"I want you to double your efforts," she said. "Find him. Find him now."

"Not sure how to do that without any new leads," he said.

"Then find a new one," she said, and feeling a crushing weight on her chest she rose. "Find him."

She marched off, headed back to her office, and collapsed in the chair. Throughout the day, she thumbed through reports, proofread the faked documents from the graphic designer in Osaka, even carefully adding a few typos to make it look more genuine. She read the reports on the Russian memes, highlighted comments on the latest podcast episode of *The Unknown Journal*, listening to it at double-speed, and got lost in the work.

At least, she tried to, but the weight kept getting heavier as the day stretched into evening.

Athena stared at her conspiracy wall, focused on an image of Mitchell at the center with strings connecting him to various documents, spreadsheets, and sticky-notes. She pulled several push-pins setting the photo of Mitchell free from the wall, and gently placed it on her desk. She stared at it, unable to think.

It was hours later when she realized she hadn't eaten, sitting at her computer, and she heard the familiar chime of the forum alert.

She sat upright in her chair, and scanned the titles of the various tabs open in her browser until she came to The Kitty Hawk Conspiracy thread.

She read the message from Mitchell's username and felt a wash of excitement, guilt, and relief.

Gemini, it read. *Are you there? I figured it out. We need to meet. It's worse than I imagined.*

Athena typed as fast as she could. *Are you alright? Where are you?*

Mitchell's words came a few moments later. *This chat room may not be safe. Do you like puzzles?*

Athena typed back, amused. *Of course I do,* she wrote.

She felt her heart in her throat as the three dots scrolled

across the chat window indicating he was typing. The wait felt eternal.

I'm at a motel. My wife made a list of chores for me. Come as soon as you can.

Athena leaned back in her chair, and opened a fresh browser window. A quick search later, and she had the address of a roadside motel, the Honey Dew Motel, some fifty miles away from Mitchell's house.

"Honey-Do list," she said, shaking her head and smiling despite herself. "Amateur."

— **6.4** —

It was after ten o'clock the next night when she pulled up to a run-down, two-story motel on a forgotten highway. Whatever charm it might have once held was long ago replaced with rust and peeling paint. Athena wondered how long it had been since the entirety of the neon on the sign for the Honey Dew Motel had worked.

She rolled into the parking lot and saw a light on in a second-floor window. Other than the lights on the exterior and the singular lamp on in the office, it was the only sign of life.

"Here we go," she said. "God help me."

She braced herself, she wasn't sure what was going to happen. When she'd first met Mitchell at the Rosewater, she hadn't bothered to worry. He'd seemed harmless enough, and she had Howell nearby. But after her encounter with his wife, and his disappearance, she didn't want to come unprepared. She pulled the mace from her purse, and got out of her car.

Athena made her way up the creaking stairs, and carefully approached the door with the light on. She heard someone shuffle on the other side of the door, causing a clatter.

She gave a gentle knock to the door.

"Mitchell?" she called, her heart racing and her hand tightening on her mace.

Shuffling footsteps approached the door and what sounded like the rattle of cans came from the other side. There was a screech of metal, something being dragged across the floor with some effort. She couldn't imagine what that was.

"Mitchell? Are you okay?" she said again, pleading. "It's me. It's Gemini. Can you hear me? Please tell me you're okay."

The door cracked open as far as the security chain would allow and Mitchell appeared, leaning in with several day's growth of beard. The flicker of light she had seen was the muted television. Athena noticed something glittering on the walls behind him, and the mixed odor of rotten food, mildew, and body odor hit her. Mitchell himself looked and smelled like he hadn't showered in days. She choked back a gag.

"No," he interrupted himself with a cough. "No-nobody saw you come here, did they?"

"I wasn't followed," she assured him, thinking back on their first face-to-face where she'd asked the same thing.

"Y-you're sure," he asked. She caught him touching the pale stripe of scar tissue along his temple.

"There's no one here but me, Mitchell," she promised. "I swear to you."

"You wouldn't lie to me, would you?" He was shaking. "You wouldn't, you wouldn't." The words became a mantra he muttered repeatedly under his breath.

Athena braced herself, her hand tightening on her mace. "I couldn't."

The door slammed shut, and Athena jumped back. After a rattle of its chain, the door slowly opened to reveal a chaotic sprawl of sixteen day's worth of food boxes, beer cans, and stacks of papers. Everything was arranged in stacks. The mattresses and the bed were placed against the wall, creating a kind of barricade. The screech she had heard was the dresser being pulled across the floor away from the door.

The rest of the furniture was stacked on top of each other against the window. The chairs were tucked into each other and carefully balanced on the nightstand. There were stains on the wall — more accurately the absence of stains — where the paintings had been removed and arranged in the corner, like a house of cards. The bed frames leaned against each other making a metal tent with a nest of wadded-up blankets inside.

The light from the television showed the source of the glittering she had seen from outside. The entire ceiling was covered in aluminum foil, held in place by stuffing it into the ceiling tile panels and silver gaffer's tape. She could see in his work where he had run out of covering the entirety of the walls and filled the rest with strategically placed stripes.

"Oh, shit," she said, stepping back.

"Hurry," he gestured, "before someone sees you!"

"I'm sorry," she turned to run, but he grabbed her arm. She whipped around to spray him, but he immediately let go.

"I'm s-sorry," he said, pulling his arm back. "I shouldn't have done that. But, I have to show you. I get it now. I know what it is."

He moved away from her and opened the door fully. He took a few steps back into the motel room, and beckoned for her to follow. Despite her lizard brain demanding that she run, she instead found herself stepping forward. Her hand still gripped the mace tightly.

"What is this?" she stared at the mess of the room.

"This is what I've been doing," he said. "It's taken me a while, but I finally figured it out. Putting it together one piece at a time. I printed everything I could out at work until they busted me. I can't afford to go on the forums anymore. I'm worried they'll track me. So I printed it all out and came back here."

"Who's 'they?'" she asked.

Mitchell stared at her in disbelief. "What do you mean, 'who's they'?" he asked. Then, he added as if the answer was obvious, "Those behind Glowaski, whoever's building the Kitty Hawk. I haven't found their names yet, so I'm just calling them the Carolinas, for now. Glowaski's just a front, right? Or a patsy. The Carolinas have gone through a lot of trouble to hide their secret, but I figured it out."

Mitchell rummaged through the documents and pulled up the first document she created; the one he found under the placemat at the Starlight Diner.

He pointed to the logo in the corner. "Project Carolina. It's not what I thought. They say it can break the speed of light barrier and they call it a Hadron Drive, but what they call it isn't important. It's what it does that matters. And that's not all, it's got breakthroughs in wireless energy transfer. Do you know what that means?"

Athena tried to control her emotions. To find herself in the Gemini character again. "Tell me."

"It came to me," he said, "when I tried to explain it to Danny. Since then, it's all come together. What does Glowaski do? Why them? What are they up to? It means that not only is NASA working on a ship capable of faster-than-light travel, but something bigger."

Athena shook her head, and took a half-step back. "I don't know, Mitchell," she said. Her mind raced to figure out how to derail him and bring him back to reality.

"These photos," he snatched a stack of images from the pile, "I pulled these from the Glowaski site. They're about that crash that happened a few weeks ago, but if you look closely you can tell that they're doctored. You have to adjust the levels in the photo so you can see it. The pixel pattern doesn't quite match. They've altered them to hide this."

"They," she said. "The Carolinas." Athena examined Mitchell's printed photo of the crash. He'd highlighted the parts they had intentionally blurred so that they could hide further clues. He handed her the picture of the base of Saturn that the designer in Osaka had done.

"The government does that all the time. Look at this. Tell me the government isn't hiding something. There's a perfectly symmetrical hexagon on the base of Saturn? I don't think so. Tell me that's a natural occurrence."

"But what is this?" she asked. "What do you think this all means?"

Mitchell's words came out in a frantic blur. "It's from Saturn, Gemini. I can prove it, I can."

"Saturn?" Athena said, genuinely surprised. She set the photos aside, and watched him as he paced back and forth like an animal in a cage.

"It's absolutely incredible and I have proof," he said. His hands shook as he gesticulated wildly as he paced. "This ship that crashed, it somehow uses an artificial black hole as a gravity sail."

He held up a printout of the schematic, the same one Athena had commissioned.

"This spire on the nose?" he pointed to the schematic, jabbing it with his finger. "I figured out the redacted parts. There's a pattern to it. I can see it. That spire, it generates a small black hole in front of the ship that lasts for only a fraction of a second, but the gravity it generates is enough to compress space and time. It pulls it faster than light."

"What?" she had no idea where he was going with this.

Mitchell shook with excitement. "It breaks the laws of physics, Gem." He turned, kicking around the trash that accumulated on the floor. "It breaks the goddamned laws of physics. The black hole sail is going to revolutionize the space program. But the Arclight? God, that's something terrifying."

His hands moved faster, snapping his fingers as he talked. His wild eyes darted back and forth as he shuffled through the stacks of papers.

"Oh, Mitchell," she said, in her mind she pleaded for him to stop.

"I-imagine," he stammered, then collected himself. His eyes still burned with a manic fire. "Imagine an engine that can generate infinite power with nothing more than a scrap of matter. Now, imagine directing that energy wirelessly."

A dark realization hit her.

"A weapon," she said. "You think it's a weapon."

Mitchell snapped his fingers, signaling that she was right. "Yes! That's why Glowaski. They have the resources. The connections. They've made something absolutely invisible. Absolutely untraceable. With a wavelength so narrow, it can virtually pass through solid objects to get to its target. It can be shot from space at the push of a button. The entire drone program was created just as a diversion from Kitty Hawk. They could kill me for just saying this, Gem. You get that, right? And they can do it from space in the blink of an eye. That's why I did this." He waved his hands to the ceiling covered in aluminum foil. "To protect it from seeing me. From finding me."

Athena heard her voice crack. "Oh, I'm so sorry, Mitchell. I can't."

His expression darkened. "Aren't you listening? What do you mean, 'I can't,'" he said. "That's why I needed you to understand. We're in danger. We blow the whistle on this, we're dead. You understand me? We're dead. Anyone who's ever seen this document is dead. Oh, god," he stopped. His hands went to his face. "I told my wife. What if they think she knows? Do I warn her?"

"Mitchell?" she said. "You have to stop this, please."

Mitchell shook his head. "No, no, no, we shouldn't stop. I can't. We can't. Wait. Wait, wait, wait. No, we have to tell everyone. It's our only chance. If everyone knows, they'll have no reason to come after us. Do you know what this means? This changes everything!"

Athena felt on the verge of tears. "I did this," she whispered. "This is my fault."

"What?" Mitchell didn't understand. "What do you mean?"

How could he understand? Athena wondered.

"What do you mean? No, it's not your fault. It can't be. None of this is your fault," he said. "It was your documents that pointed me to the truth. You opened my eyes. You are my angel in this. Without you, I couldn't have uncovered it. I should thank you."

"None of this is real," she said, her eyes wet.

"I don't understand," he said. "I thought you'd be happy. This is why they killed your husband."

She turned to the door. "I have to go."

Mitchell took a step back, as if betrayed. "Gem," he said. "You can't."

"My name is Athena," she said. "Please, Mitchell, you have to stop this. You have to forget everything. You have to go home to your wife. Get your life back."

"She didn't understand. Danielle didn't understand, but you do," he said. "We can figure this out together. I know it. We have to figure out how to tell everyone. We tell everyone, they can't get all of us, can they?"

"I can't be part of this anymore," she said. "I'm sorry."

"You have to be," he said. His hand lashed out and closed around her arm. "You can't go, Gem," he said. "It's not safe."

"Let me go, Mitchell," she raised her mace. "Don't make me hurt you."

His eyes went from his hand to her eyes, as if he hadn't realized what he was doing. He saw her try to switch the mace from the hand he was holding to her free one. His grip tightened.

"But, you're the only other one who saw it, too," he said. "You've seen it with your own eyes. You're part of this. You're the only one who can verify the sighting!"

Athena pulled her arm free and headed to the door. She held her mace up. "I'm leaving. Now!"

"Don't go!" he growled, and lunged for her. Athena brought the mace up, only to have it fumble from her hand. She backed away, hitting the wall and feeling the strip of aluminum foil crinkle as she hit it. She didn't dare take her eyes off of him. Her hand pawed until she found the door frame, and ran.

"Gemini!" he shouted.

Athena raced down the stairs, nearly tripping over herself as she made it down. On the last step, she craned her neck to see him leaning against the railing on second floor. His eyes were filled with fear and rage.

Her footing slipped, and she hit the ground hard. She barely broke her fall; her head bounced off the ground. Her hands already stung from the asphalt of the parking lot. She felt something loose in her mouth and spat out a piece of tooth. She could taste her mouth filling with blood.

Mitchell called from the railing. "She kicked me out," he shouted. "Danielle told me to leave, so I did. I haven't seen my daughter in weeks. This is all I have. It has to mean something or all of this has been for nothing!"

She threw the car door open, tasting the blood in her mouth. She managed to get the car started, and she slammed her foot on the accelerator, leaving the Honey Dew Motel in her rearview. She heard Mitchell let out a rage-filled howl just as she made it to the highway.

She made it about a mile before she had to pull over. She was hyperventilating. She was bleeding. She got out, spat out a mouthful of blood, and likely a piece of tooth, and tried to get her breathing under control.

She slammed her hand on the hood of her car, and let out a primal scream of her own.

"What have I done?" she asked herself. But she knew exactly what she had done, and it sickened her.

CHAPTER SEVEN
THE LIGHTBULB GOES OUT

— 7.1 —

"Shame on you for just willfully ignoring what"s right in front of you," Cavanaugh said to Mad Autumn.

"With all due, Ms. Cavanaugh," Mad Autumn said. "I think you're the one who's in denial."

The image on the screen was that of a 3500-year-old relief sculpture from the Hathor Temple in Egypt. It showed a man holding a long, round orb, propped up by some kind of apparatus. Inside the orb, a writhing snake slithered in its center, looking for all the world like wire filament. At its end, there was a lotus flower with its stem curling around as if it were some kind of cable. It was known as the Dendera Light, and in other circles it was simply known as the Egyptian Lightbulb. It was a favorite of those who believed that aliens had anything to do with the building of the pyramids, and proof of advanced technology in ancient Egypt.

And, like, everything else she had been forced to sit through this evening, it was complete nonsense.

"No," Cavanaugh sighed, "ancient Egyptians didn't have lightbulbs, and shame on you for ignoring every other similar depiction of the lotus flower and the Egyptian creation myth because a singular carving of the myth kind-of-sort-of looks like it could be a lightbulb. If it were, there would be literally any physical evidence of the actual artifact. Glass, wire, anything. But there isn't."

Stanislav whipped around to Cavanaugh. "Then how do you explain that there is no torch soot on the roof of the passage ways in any of the Pyramids of Egypt?"

"Well," Mad Autumn taunted.

"First of all," she said, "the temple in question did, in fact, have centuries of torch soot on the ceiling. Second of all, I'm pretty sure there wasn't much soot in the pyramids because it's more likely they used reflectors to bounce light to see. And did you know that salting torches lessened torch-black? The ancient Egyptians knew. I know, too, because I looked it up."

Both Gerry Henry and Stanislav shared a derisive rolling of their eyes.

Cavanaugh continued, "They also built the pyramids from the inside out, one layer at a time, where they could see what they're doing as they built it. Setting the edge stones and filling in the rest. I know, because I also looked that up. Or do you want to just ignore any archeological findings that are counter to your forgone conclusion? Or did your psychic premonitions and visions tell you how the pyramids were built?"

Stanislav crossed his arms. He was not interested. The man was all but pouting.

"I thought so," she said. "This so-called lightbulb, this evidence of advanced technology in ancient history, isn't what you say it is. The lotus flower and the snake represent fertility and the flooding of the Nile respectively. I know, because, again, I looked it up."

— 7.2 —

"Ladies and Gentlemen," Franklin said, sending the cork of the champagne flying across the Roswell conference room. "We've done good work, and I couldn't be prouder of all of you. The project has taken on a life of its own, and the community has embraced the Carolina documents and Codename: Kitty Hawk as absolute fact."

Franklin stood in front of Athena's team. Behind him on the screen was the Project: Carolina seal from the faked documents. Across the seal was a logo that read 'Closed.' A little graphic that one of her designers had thrown together for the occasion, though there would be ongoing work for the upkeep of the project for months if not years to come.

Athena sat in the conference seat at the end of the table, arms crossed, and staring at nothing while Franklin addressed the small crowd of agents and designers that were under her charge.

"Agencies for the Chinese, the Koreans, the Iranians, the Russians, Germans, and even the Brits, are all scrambling like mad to stay on top of this," he said, beaming with pride. "They're trying to figure out what we're *really* up to."

He passed the bottle to Howell, who was pouring small, measured amounts of champagne into clear, plastic cups. "This work will never be recognized formally," Franklin said. He grabbed two glasses, raised one, and made his way towards her. "The work we do here, we do for the benefit of our great nation. And the work we do, we can never share. Never take credit for. But we did good today. All of you. Never, never doubt that. What you have done, is create a new mythology. Something that will be talked about for decades to come. I, for one, couldn't be prouder of you."

Franklin offered one of the cups to Athena. "Don't worry," he assured her. "It's non-alcoholic." and then raised his own in salute, turning towards the rest of the room.

"To the architect of this tale, Athena Simms," he shouted. "To the Carolina Papers and the Kitty Hawk team! And to our next victory!"

The rest of the team broke into applause and cheers. Athena forced a smile, and downed the cup after the slightest of salutes. But she was unable to make eye contact with anyone. Not Franklin. Not Bugs. Not even Howell. All she felt was an emptiness. The applause faded, as she rose from her seat and crossed the conference room and stormed out the door.

The others stared, confused.

She balled her fists, and made her way through the offices to the war room.

Athena stared at the conspiracy work board she had used to map out the operation. At its center, the smiling image of Mitchell Vincent taken from his employer's website. But all she could see was the man he'd become, holed up in the Honey Dew, hiding in shadows.

Athena grabbed the corner of her wall and angrily ripped apart her work with a scream. She sensed someone behind her, and she turned to see Franklin leaning in the doorway.

"I warned you," he said. "I warned you not to get too personally involved. I warned you to stay detached. I warned you to learn from my mistakes."

Athena collapsed into one of the conference chairs. She sank as deep as she could in the chair, not wanting to meet his gaze.

"And once again, you put yourself in an unnecessary situation," Franklin said, then, his tone eased. "How's the tooth, by the way? Is everything all right?"

"I want to call it off," she said. Her mouth still hurt from the emergency dental work that morning. The flight home had been brutal. She had barely made it until morning, spitting blood into a plastic cup until she was able to get to her dentist.

Franklin had called six times while she was getting treated. Now, a temporary crown sat over her chipped tooth and her cheek still tingled from the local anesthetic.

Franklin closed the door, and sat in a chair opposite her. He studied her, concerned. He steepled his fingers. "And what does that mean to you, exactly, 'to call it off?'"

"Mitchell Vincent," she began, "he's lost it. Just lost it. He's holed up in a motel room, having covered every square inch of the place with aluminum foil and — "

"That's great!" Franklin exclaimed.

"It's not," she said, unable to believe what she was hearing. "It's so far from great. We destroyed him. I destroyed him."

"Remind me what the goal was here, Simms," he said.

Athena couldn't meet his gaze. "To get him to believe in something fantastic."

"Exactly," he said. "To tell a story. To get him to believe in what you've created. Your story. That's the job. And you did it *great*. That FTL stuff? Fantastic. We're using it on the new Holiday-Utah Project. You did more than tell a story; you created a movement."

"He's broken," she said. "His family's broken. And it's my fault. It's all my fault. I have to tell him."

Franklin raised his hand, signaling her to stop. "So," he said, cooly, "let's chalk that statement up to, 'I want to say this out loud just to hear it, but I'd never in million years follow through with it.'"

"Why can't we?" she asked.

Franklin adjusted his tie. "Because it'd be considered

the revelation of State Secrets and treason, that's why," he said, matter of factly. "Don't feel bad because you did your job well, Simms. Not for a second. This is exactly the reaction we wanted. He's in. The store's empty because he bought everything. It's a magic trick where he's listening to the patter and not looking at the hand palming the ball. His friends are in. The forums are exploding. The Kitty Hawk Conspiracy will be talked about for years."

"What have I done?" she whispered.

"Your job," he said. "And let me remind you what that is. Your job here is, and always has been, to lie, deceive, misdirect, and to serve the greater good by protecting the secrets of the United States of America. Has there been some miscommunication here? Have I not been clear from the beginning about this?"

"I can't," she said. "Not anymore."

"You know what? Let's cool it with this case for a couple weeks. We'll get Cleveland to watch the project for a while. Let's get you on something a little less personal." He gestured to one of the boards in his office filled with bits of paper pinned to a cork board. "We have some fake fusion schematics we need someone to go over. You want me to switch you over to that?"

"I'm sorry," she rose from her seat. "I just can't. I've spent the last five weeks leading him by the nose. Promising answers just out of reach. And he went from this sweet, family man with a quirk to I-don't-know-what."

Franklin thought for a moment. "Take some time off, Simms," he said. His tone was oddly paternal. "Get out of your own head. We have still have much more work to do.

This guy — "

"Mitchell Vincent," Athena snapped. "We destroyed his life, the least you could do is remember his name."

"You're out of line," he said with just a hint of anger.

"You owe him that."

"I don't owe him anything," Franklin said. "And neither do you. You're a soldier now, Simms. And you're brilliant at it. I don't use that word lightly. You want to feel bad about something, feel bad about the fact I don't have an army of you."

"But," she began, but Franklin tilted his head, and she knew enough about him to read his body language and stay quiet.

"Now," he said, his tone growing darker and darker as he spoke, "you have two choices. You can get back to work — work that you do exceedingly well, by the way — or you can leave and prepare yourself for the inevitable consequences of that decision."

Athena met Franklin's gaze and swallowed, unsure what she was going to do. There was no mistaking the darkness of his words. No telling what he would do to her.

"Sir, yes, sir," she said, finally, and counted the seconds until she could get back on a plane to Arizona.

— 7.3 —

Danielle pulled back the curtain just enough to see Gemini-Mary-whatever-her-name approaching the house. She'd seen the blue compact car roll into her driveway, and prepared herself. The same woman she'd seen at the Starlight Diner was dressed in a black jacket and jeans approaching the house hesitantly. When Danielle answered the quiet knock at the door, she found the woman standing on her porch with a pleading look in her eyes. She was fairly certain the woman couldn't see the pistol Danielle had behind her back. It was Mitchell's and she'd only ever fired it once, in practice.

Of the flood of emotions that hit her, anger was the one that Danielle latched onto.

"You have about five seconds to get off my property before I call the cops, or just decide to shoot you for trespassing," Danielle said.

"I know I have no right to be here," the woman, Gemini, said. "Mitchell's not well. You have to help him."

Danielle sized her up. "I don't care."

Gemini shook her head. "I hope that's not true," she said. "You cared for him once, and he needs you now."

"I can't help him," Danielle said. "Not if he doesn't want to be helped. God knows I tried over the years."

"If you love him — "

Danielle slammed the door in her face, and turned away, feeling the weight of the pistol in her hands.

"If you love him," Gemini called through the door,

"please help him."

Danielle opened the door again, this time not bothering to hide the pistol. "Who are you?" she demanded. "Really?"

Seeing the gun in Danielle's hand, the woman's eyes went wide. She stepped back and held up her hands, trying to appear non-threatening. "I-I'm just someone who wants to do the right thing."

Danielle's hand tightened on her pistol. It was still low against her thigh. She wasn't sure what she would do if she brought it up to actually aim it at the woman.

"The right thing, huh?" she asked. Then a realization hit her about this mouse of a woman in front of her, an undeniable truth. "You did this to him, didn't you? Somehow you're responsible for all this. Somehow this is *your* fault."

Gemini winced at Danielle's words. She took another step back. Danielle wondered if the woman would try to run, and what she would do if the woman did.

"I tried to tell him to come home," she said. "I tried. I really did."

Danielle growled, "Where is he?"

Gemini pulled a piece of paper out of her pocket and set it on the porch. With both hands raised, she backed away trembling. Danielle opened it up to find the name and address of some rathole motel about an hour's drive away.

"At a motel called the Honey Dew," she said. "Room 22. He's been there for weeks."

Danielle crumpled the paper into a ball. Despite her rage, worry began to creep into her. She asked, "Is he okay?"

Gemini shook her head. "I don't think so," she said. "I don't think he's okay at all."

"What's he doing?" Danielle asked.

"He's there waiting to be killed, I think," the woman said. "He thinks 'they' are after him." Danielle noticed that Gemini was inching ever closer to her car, not taking her eyes off the gun in her hand.

"Are you?" Danielle studied her. "Are you after him?"

Her eyes went to Danielle. "None of this was supposed to happen," she said. "I swear I never meant for any of this to go this far. You have to help him."

"Why did you do it then?" Danielle asked.

"I didn't mean to," she said, lowering her head. "He seemed like a good man."

"He was," Danielle said, "but that was before you showed up." With that, Danielle backed into the house and closed the door again.

Once Gemini's car was out of sight, Danielle finally set the pistol down, and called for her daughter. It was time for a trip North.

— 7.4 —

Hours later, with Allie safely at her mother's, Danielle arrived at the Honey Dew Motel with her stomach eating itself. She'd pulled open the glove compartment to see the pistol sitting there, and decided to leave it there. Even at his most manic, Mitchell would never hurt her. But, she'd been worried enough to bring it. She opened the car door and had to use the rusted hand rail to steady her steps up to the second floor.

She found Room 22 easily enough, and stood outside the door daring herself to knock. The whole drive here she'd run over the possibilities of what to say in her head. She didn't know what to expect, but, her experience told her to prepare for the worst.

Gemini-Mary had been right about one thing. She had to try. She'd pulled Mitchell back from the brink before, maybe she could do it again. Danielle braced herself and knocked on the door.

She heard movement, but no answer.

"Mitchell?" she knocked again. "Are you in there? It's me. It's Danny."

She heard someone shuffling from inside the motel room, and out of the corner of her eye saw a flicker of motion in the thick curtains that blocked her view of what was inside.

"You have to come out," she said. "I just want to talk."

She heard the rattle of the chain, and felt her heart sink as the door cracked open as far as the chain would allow.

When she saw Mitchell, she saw a hollow shell of the man she knew. His eyes were bloodshot, narrowed in suspicion, and rapidly moving around in their sockets. His shirt was a mess, covered in stains. His face was thin. His shoulders were slumped as if the very act of standing was taking all the strength he had. The smell from the room was one of rot.

"How did you find me?" he asked with a mix of elation and disbelief in his voice. "Are you," he started, then centered himself, "real?"

Danielle held her breath, unsure what to say. "A woman came to see me," she said, once she was able to find the words. "Gemini, she told me that you weren't well."

His eyes darted around her. "Where's Allie?" he asked, switching from suspicious to panicked.

"With Mother," Danielle assured him. "She's safe, I promise. Now, open the door, Mitchell, please. I want to talk. Whatever this is, we can get through it."

"I'm afraid," he admitted. "I'm afraid you're going to get hurt. That Allie would," he trailed off, and appeared to be struggling with himself. It was as if he were forcing himself to put his thoughts together. "If you knew what I know, they might come after you. I can't let that happen. I'm doing this to protect you."

"It won't happen, Mitchell," she said. "There's no one after you."

Mitchell recoiled as if slapped. "No," he said. "They are. They're watching my every move. That's why I had to go into hiding. You don't understand, this is for you. For Allie."

"You're right, I don't understand," Danielle said. "But I want to. I just want my husband back."

Mitchell pressed himself against the door, staring blankly at her. "What do you mean?"

"You're a sweet man," she said. "You're just lost and I want you to find your way home. I just don't know what to do anymore. This alien thing — "

"This is not just some *thing!* " he shouted. He slammed his fist on the wall, and Danielle jumped back.

"It's not, honey," she put her hand on the wall next to door, as if to touch him. "It never was. None of it."

"Don't," he pleaded. "Don't say that! I have proof!" His words devolved into a complex blur of thoughts as he moved around the room, and she could see inside enough to get a glimpse of the stacks of food boxes, the strangely-stacked furniture, and the thing that broke her heart, the aluminum foil glittering on the ceiling.

"Oh, god," she whispered. Danielle realized the fight was finally over, and she'd lost. Mitchell continued to ramble, but Danielle couldn't listen anymore.

"You have a video of some lights," she said, just above a whisper. "That's all. They're just lights, Mitchell. They're just lights."

Mitchell's face went ashen. "They got to you, didn't they?" he asked. "Did they come to the house? Did they hurt you? Are they threatening you?"

"Nobody hurt me," she said. "Nobody got to me. But, it doesn't seem like I can get to you, either."

"They're building a weapon," he said through the crack

in the door. "A terrible weapon. I know how it sounds, but it's true. I-I swear. They've — "

"They're not," she said. Exhausted, Danielle felt her entire body give way, like she was going to collapse. "She lied to you, Mitchell. The woman. Somehow she was part of it. She told me, it's all a lie."

Mitchell's lip quivered. "That's not true," he said. "It can't be."

"It is," Danielle said. "She came to me and she asked me to find you because she felt guilty. Whoever she is, she wanted you to come home. I don't know what she told you, but I bet not a word of it was true."

"This has to be some kind of trick," he growled. He slammed the door, and she heard him roar in rage, frustration, panic.

"I know you're scared, but I don't know how to help you anymore," she called through the door. "I've done everything I know to do and it's just not enough. Talk to me, Mitch. What more can I do? "

"I don't know," he admitted, through the closed door. "They must have gotten to her, too. Part of their plan. To get her to get to you, to get to me." He was silent for a moment, and gasped. "They know where I am. I'm not safe anymore!"

"You have to want help." *One last plea,* she thought. *One last chance, Mitchell. Please take it.* "Do you?"

Silence came from the other side of the door.

"Just open the door and we can try again," she said. "Forget all of this. Forget whatever this is and focus on something that matters."

"Then what does?" he snapped. "What matters, Danielle?"

"You do," she said, not believing she had to say it out loud. "Come out, Mitch, please. I don't want to end like this. You and me yelling at each other through a door. Really?"

Please take it.

"What do you mean?" he asked nervously. "End?"

"You know what I mean," she said. "I can't live like this anymore. I can't live my life worried that you might go off again. That you might hurt yourself. Or me. Or Allie."

"I'd never," he said.

"I want to help you, but you won't let me," she said. "But if you don't even trust me enough to open this door, I can't see how we can continue this."

"Danny?"

Danielle steeled herself. "I'll give you to the count of three. Just open the door, Mitchell. That's all I ask. I love you. That has to mean something, right?"

"Don't," he said.

"One."

"Danielle?"

"Two."

"Please. I can't," he said. "I can't leave. If I do, they'll know where I am. They'll track us down. Hunt us like animals."

Danielle whispered, "Three."

She backed away, pulling the wedding ring from her

finger. She laid the ring at the base of the door, and cried all the way down the stairs, not realizing it would be the last time she would ever see Mitchell Vincent alive again.

— 7.5 —

The last time she was here, at the Rosewater, Athena Simms sat across from Mitchell in this very booth, and handed him a file folder filled with documents that she had written, art directed, and crumpled up to make them appear to be aged.

She swirled ice cubes in her glass, and downed the last of her third glass of Uncle Nearest on the rocks.

God, she thought as the haze of the whiskey started to cloud her mind, *this tastes amazing.*

A large man slid into the booth across from her. The last time he had been here, he'd worn a fake mustache and a hoodie. Now, Howell wore his gray suit and thin tie.

The two questions that crossed her rapidly-blurring mind were, did he know what she'd done, and what was he going to do to her?

"How's it going, soldier?" he asked.

"Don't call me that," she said. "And badly. Things are going badly."

Howell signaled to the bartender for a drink. "We all have bad days."

"Did Franklin send you here to intimidate me?" she slurred. "To scare me back into line? Because he did a pretty good job of that back at the office."

"Honestly, Franklin's worried about you," Howell said.

Athena laughed, nearly spitting out her drink. "What!"

"He sent me to ask you to come back," he said.

"Or what?" she said. "Or else?"

The bartender, a weathered, lanky man with his long black hair pulled into a ponytail, approached and set down a beer in front of Howell, saving him from having to answer. The contrast between the two, the tatted man in the black v-neck tee and the man who looked like he stepped out of a 1950s police show, caused Athena to giggle despite knowing Howell was right in front of her.

Howell held the glass with both hands but did not take a drink. Perhaps he just didn't want to appear any more conspicuous than necessary, as if wearing a suit in a dive bar wasn't conspicuous enough. Howell stared at it, and Athena could see his gears turning.

Athena took the opportunity, swirled the ice cubes in her glass and raised it to the bartender. "Another, please, handsome?"

"You got it." Giving her a half-grin, the bartender took the glass and headed back to his station.

When she was certain the bartender was out of earshot, she asked. "What would they do?"

Howell's posture somehow got straighter. "What do you expect them to do?"

Athena leaned in and whispered, "A shadow intelligence

CHAD ALLAN JONES

agency dedicated to falsifying information to protect their secrets? I expect them to send out their most handsome agent to buy a girl a drink."

"I think that can be arranged," he said, raising his glass in salute.

"All of 'em, by the way," she said. "All the drinks. I have some lost time to make up, you know." Athena leaned back and tapped her fingers on the table, thinking. "I really don't have a choice, do I?"

"Of course you do," he said. "But, will you make the smart one? Smart people don't always do smart things. And I'm here to ask the smartest woman I've ever met to not do something stupid."

Athena gave the bartender a warm smile as he set down another glass of whiskey and ice. She knocked it back and smiled, downing most of it in one gulp.

"What do you tell people you do, when they ask?"

"The truth," he admitted. "That it's classified."

Athena raised her nearly empty glass in a half-hearted salute, and they clinked glasses.

"To the truth!" Athena shouted and drained the rest of her drink, and felt the warmth of it in her throat.

"I'm not going to lie," she said. "Feels good to be drunk again. Damn good." Athena signaled the bartender for another drink, and batted her eyes.

Howell took the smallest of sips from his beer before setting it back on the table and easing it to the side. He folded his hands in front of Athena. "How long's it been?" he asked with concern in his voice. "If you don't mind," he added.

Athena locked eyes with his and took a deep breath. "You ever kill a man, Smiles?"

Howell stiffened; she'd struck a nerve.

"It's been seven years since I got behind the wheel when I shouldn't have and killed a man," she said. "Seven years and I can still hear the crunch when I hit him. I can still feel it, like a phantom pain. Seven years since I walked away on a technicality. Seven years since it ruined me. Sorry, that's past tense. I'm still ruined."

Howell sat in silence for nearly a minute.

"You don't know what to say to that, do you?" she asked.

"No," he admitted. "I don't."

"It's okay. I don't either," she said, managing a smile, and felt her throat tense. A new wave of sorrow came crashing on her. "This job, is it always like this?"

"Some you win. Some you lose," he said. "This one? Whether you believe it or not, we won."

Athena wiped away a tear. "Sure doesn't feel like it. How do I know if I did the right thing?"

"That's easy," he said. "There's no 'right thing' here. There's just various degrees of wrong."

"I just thought I had this amazing opportunity to do something important," she said. "To use my talents for something greater than myself. And what did I do with it? I destroyed a man. Why? Because I needed a paycheck. Because I didn't think about the consequences. Because I thought it would be a challenge. Because I thought it would be fun."

Athena reached over and took his beer, and swallowed most of it in one gulp, barely tasting it. She only stopped because she needed air. "Oh, I'm going to be sick tonight," she promised.

Howell took the glass from her hand. "It may not seem this way right now, but you did a good thing."

"Lying to people is a good thing?" she asked.

"It is when it's to keep a secret," he said. "A secret worth hundreds of billions in technology and hardware. When it's for the greater good."

"And what's that?" Then, she added mockingly, "The greater good."

"What we do, it's weird," Howell said, "but it's important. The boss is playing the strangest game of chess in the intelligence community."

"Does that make me his pawn?" she snorted.

"No, ma'am," he said. "You're his queen. The most powerful piece on the board." Howell took her hands. She didn't realize they were trembling until he did. His hands were warm, and had a calming effect on her nerves.

"Why, Smiles, are you hitting on me?" she asked, with more than a hint of sarcasm. She pulled away, she didn't deserve any consolation. She didn't deserve his worry.

"Not that I'm aware of," Howell said, suddenly off balance.

"Good," she said. "Because my self-esteem isn't that low yet. Come back after about two more drinks. Then we'll see if I've had enough to drink you pretty."

Howell let out a laugh.

"You know how I got this job?" she asked. Howell shook his head, a curious expression on his face.

"My agent got me into this think tank project," she said. "Quick little job for the government. Writers and engineers and hackers and artists. And our job was to imagine worst-case scenarios. Think like a terrorist, like a monster. That was the gig. And, who knew, I was apparently really, really good at it. I was a natural. That's how I got on Franklin's radar. But, I could never have imagined anything worse than how I feel right now."

"I don't know if this will help." Howell took his glass back from her. "But, a guy believes with all his heart that there are aliens out there, working with the government to do god knows what. How sane did you really think he'd be?"

Athena fidgeted with her empty glass, and thought about Mitchell. "He's not crazy, you know."

"Then what is he?"

"Just someone who just needs something to believe in," Athena said. "We all are."

They sat there for hours, and she had a vague memory of Howell driving her back to her hotel, and easing her fully clothed into bed. She remembered only patting him on the cheek, and passing out.

The next morning, she woke up face down in her hotel bathroom, covered in her own sick as promised. She had a spectacular hangover, and an absolute certainty of what she would do next.

She would run.

And never look back.

CHAPTER EIGHT

LAST NIGHT OF THE CON

— 8.1 —

When the last of the audience questions had been answered, and the slide that read, 'The End,' came up on the screen behind the dais, the room broke out into a polite applause as Mad Autumn shuffled her note cards at her podium. For her part, Mad Autumn was exhausted and very much looking forward to the day coming to an end so that the partying could begin.

"Well," she said, giving Cavanaugh an over-dramatic sigh. "We've certainly been given a lot to think about. This concludes our panel, but before we do — "

"Before we do," Cavanaugh interrupted, leaning forward into her mic, "One more question, this one for the audience."

Mad Autumn shrugged. "Unorthodox, but okay."

"Alright, show of hands," she called to the crowd. "After all you've heard today, how many of you still believe that aliens have shaped the course of human history?"

Not surprised, Mad Autumn surveyed the audience and one-by-one, they all raised their hands. To her amusement, Margo Cavanaugh, who had been a thorn in her side for the last ninety minutes, slumped in her seat, defeated.

"Unbelievable," Cavanaugh muttered. She turned to the other panelists. "You're all a bunch of frauds you know that?" Then, to the audience she added, "You know they're a bunch of frauds, right?"

Gerry Henry leaned back, staring her down. "You call us frauds?" he said. "You say that we only ignore facts to peddle our wares. Then tell us, Ms. Cavanaugh. Why are you here, again? Your book, *Conspiracy Smith*? Peddling a piece of fiction — yes, fiction — where you deconstruct the Kitty Hawk Conspiracy, one of the most significant pieces of ufology in the twenty-first century."

"You've read it?" Cavanaugh asked, surprised.

"Enough of it to get the gist," Henry admitted. "You're not the only one who does their research. In it, you treat the Kitty Hawk Conspiracy as if it's nothing more than the fantastical tale of a delusional mind. The Kitty Hawk Conspiracy, the Arclight weapon, the Carolina documents, the Glowaski site, these are grounded evidence of modern day extraterrestrial influence. You're up here throwing out your own ad hoc evidence that supports your cause, because, I bet you think it'll sell a few extra books. There are many here that point to that find as one of the most credible pieces of evidence of government cover up of the truth. What makes you so sure that those documents were faked?"

An agreeing murmur rumbled through the VerityCon audience. Cavanaugh took a deep breath and leaned into her mic. "I can say without a doubt, there's no such thing as a Faster-Than-Light Drive Codenamed: Kitty Hawk."

"Are you so certain?" Stanislav said.

"I am."

"How?" Mad Autumn asked.

Cavanaugh took a deep breath and sighed. "Because I made it up," she said. "Because my name isn't Margo Cavanaugh. It's Athena Simms. I know, because, I was part of a secret government intelligence group whose mission was to keep the truth off balance. I was the one who wrote the Carolina papers."

The audience murmured again, this time in surprise instead of agreement. Mad Autumn saw one man in the audience who did not show any hint of surprise. A pale, gaunt man in gray with a thin scar on his temple. She had noticed him earlier, never taking his dark eyes off of Athena. Throughout the afternoon, his expression was blank and his eyes were unblinking.

"My team focused on the Carolina Project," Cavanaugh said. "I've done it so many times to so many people, I just stopped caring. And I can't live like that anymore.

"The whole of the Carolina Conspiracy is a fraud," she

continued. "I know because I oversaw its creation. I worked with a team of artists and writers to fabricate documents, directories of the Glowaski site, and faked patent filings. The Hadron-drive schematics? We based them on a vacuum cleaner turned sideways mixed with a jet engine."

Mad Autumn saw the man in gray staring at Cavanaugh flinch. His hand reached up, touching the scar on his temple.

"Impossible," Henry challenged. "I've seen the files myself. It would have taken an army of people to fake them."

"Not as many as you'd think, honestly" Cavanaugh said. "There were eight of us in all; all with the singular purpose, to misdirect the public from an experimental prototype aircraft. The group was called Augustus, and they're behind dozens of attempts to discredit anyone who's claimed to see a UFO. All of you have been lied to. And every single one of us on this dais has done it."

— 8.2 —

Athena 'Margo Cavanaugh' Simms sat at the hotel bar nursing a whiskey, sitting alone among the other convention attendees gathered in clusters around the bar. After the final panel, they were giving her a wide berth. Stanislav was holding court in a booth at the other end of the bar, surrounded by a crowd of adoring fans. She caught him doing card tricks with a tarot deck and from what she could hear, he was rambling on about famed psychic, Edgar Caycee.

Then, a wild-haired and half-drunk man dropped himself onto the seat next to her, causing her drink to rattle. He patted his hands on the bar in a drum roll. Gerry Henry had arrived.

"That was one hell of a panel," he said. "Cavanaugh, Simms, whatever you want to call yourself."

She groaned, and shot Henry a derisive glare.

"I would have pegged you for a margarita girl," he said.

"Another wholly-fabricated fact you made up."

"Oh, come on," Henry said. "Show's over. You don't have to hate us so much, you know."

Athena shrugged. "I don't have to, no. But it does pass the time."

Henry signaled to the bartender, pointing to one of the beer taps. "You're one of us," he said. "Whether you like it or not, you're part of this circus now. You're just turning out to be the saddest little clown in our little clown car."

"Oh, that's just mean," she said, pulling the cherry from her drink and biting down.

"You're so sure you're right," he said. "You are so sure that it's impossible that we've been visited. Do you have any idea how many stars — "

"Oh, stop," she cut him off. "You said it yourself. The show's over, so you can just stop it. The odds of finding life outside our planetary system is statistical certainty. The odds of it being humanoid and capable of, and, above that, interested in talking to us? Those are long, long odds, my frenemy."

Henry shrugged. "It's a big, big universe."

"Not that big," she said. "You know what gets me? I know you know what you are. I know you're just playing this… this *character* for these people. The academic who believes. What's your degree in, by the way? Right, it's in German literature, not archeology or astrophysics or anything remotely relevant to the conversation. This," she waved, gesturing up and down his frame, "is not the real you. The real you is a self-aware huckster. It's either that, or you're one-hundred percent the loon you claim to be."

"This is becoming a theme for you," he said. "You don't know what you're talking about."

"You're saying that to me?" Athena broke out in a sharp burst of laughter. "That, my dear, is irony so pure I wish I could bottle it and sell it." She raised her glass to the groups of con attendees huddled around the bar. "Because these people would apparently buy anything."

"I have to say," he said. "I do pride myself on showmanship. On knowing my audience. And that stunt you pulled back there? That was genius."

Athena paused. "What stunt?"

"Pretending to be the one behind the documents," he said. "Pretending to work for the government. *Conspiracy Smith* is good work. What I read of it, anyway. But I don't believe for a second you were the one behind the documents. I mean, points for showmanship, but, even for me, that was a leap of logic I'm not willing to make."

She took a beat to soak that in. "You...?" Athena was taken aback. "You thought that was a *stunt?*"

"Of course," Henry said. "Now, no one will believe you about anything. They'll think that even if you are a government agent, you said you made it up to protect the *real* truth about aliens." He chuckled. "Well played, Cavanaugh-Simms. Well played, indeed."

The reality of this hit Athena like a wave of cold water.

"I need another drink," she said.

Henry wrapped the bar again to get the bartender's attention. "I'm buying," he said, cheerily. "What'll you have?"

Athena waved her hand at the bottles lining the wall and said, only half-joking, "All of it."

— 8.3 —

After the pitifully-attended reading, after the disastrous panel, after the convention floor had closed for the night, and after the last call had been made at the bar, Athena had to use her hand to steady her gait through the hotel hallway back to her room. Her steps were labored, and she had to take a deep breath as the room spun, accentuating the complex spiral wallpaper pattern all around her.

She focused on a singular sound — the steady drone of electricity buzzing through the exit sign — and centered herself. She forced her eyes open, and concentrated to make sure that one foot went before the other. She realized she was stepping in the same rhythm as her heartbeat. She promised herself she wouldn't vomit, but she was not sure that was a promise she would be able to keep.

Athena was not alone in the hallway. She passed other convention goers. She was not coherent enough to hear what they were saying. She passed a couple throwing themselves at each other in mad, but awkward, passion. One struggled to get their hotel key card out of their pocket. Another, with a convention tote with the convention logo and a crudely-drawn gray alien on it slung over their shoulder nodded to Athena as she walked past.

When she got to her room, she reached into her pocket and pulled out the keycard, barely able to hang on as she awkwardly batted the keycard against the electronic lock.

Out of the corner of her eye, she saw her. Her Number One Fan, coming her way with a copy of her new book in one hand, and a marker in the other.

Athena wasn't sure how loudly she muttered the word, "Shit."

She lowered her head and forced a smile, hoping against hope the approaching fan would go past.

She didn't. "Thank you, Margo. Your book changed changed my life."

Athena leaned against the door and tried to focus on the woman. "Then, get a new one," she snapped. As she saw the woman was about to speak, she raised her hand. "Just don't."

"But," the woman began, shocked.

God help her, Athena couldn't even remember her name. Her Number One Fan, and Athena couldn't even remember her name.

"Just, get lost, go," Athena said, turning her attention back to sliding her room key into the slot.

There was a flicker of motion in her periphery. Whether or not this was her Number One Fan wandering off, or flipping her the bird, she couldn't tell. With a half-squeal of delight, she managed to get the red light on the lock to turn from red to green. With a grunt and putting her shoulder into it, she forced the door open.

She pawed for the light switch, and when she found it, she took a half-step back — both from the brightness of the light, and the ripped and torn pieces of paper scattered on the floor. Pieces of a half-finished manuscript peppered with red ink from her own notes stretched from the bed to the bathroom. But the bulk of the paper she recognized as the destroyed remains of several copies of *Confessions of a Conspiracy Smith.*

Torn to shreds.

But her world came into sharp focus when her eyes landed on the man half-engulfed in shadow sitting on the edge of one of the two beds in the room, with a gun in his hand.

Athena swallowed and felt the swell of bile rising in her throat. "Oh, shit."

The man turned towards her. He was dressed in an ill-fitting gray shirt. The last time she had seen him, he hadn't been as thin. His eyes hadn't been as sunken. His head hadn't been shaven to gray stubble. His expression hadn't been as ashen. The lines in his face hadn't been as deep.

She felt her knees give, and she barely caught herself along the wall. She wanted to run. She wanted to scream. All she could do is whisper his name.

"Mitchell?"

At his name, Mitchell Vincent's hand clenched the handle of his pistol. His eyes moved around the room from the destruction he had caused until they eventually landed on Athena.

His voice came out in a low monotone with more than a hint of menace. "Close the door."

She hesitated, turning back, willing herself to run. To take her chances on making it back to the hallway. To make her way to the lobby. But her eyes were fixed on his, and she was unsure if she would be able to make it.

"Close the door, Gemini." He lowered his head, fixed on the piece of metal in his hand. "Margo. Athena. Whatever your name is, we need to talk."

She looked back to the door, still ajar from the imperfect metal arm that failed to do its job.

Her voice broke. "Mitchell, you're not well. I — "

Mitchell cut her off with a small, almost imperceptible gesture with his pistol. He spoked in a measured, even tone, which she knew was forced. She could hear him struggling to keep his calm. His other hand was shaking.

"You're going to tell me the truth," he said. "Once and for all." Then, his calm broke into a quivering, almost sobbing. "I want to hear it from your lips. I need to hear it."

Athena, moved to the door, and instead of running —
because she could not guarantee that she would not collapse
the second she tried — she closed it. "It's not what it — "

"I know what I saw. I want the truth."

She sat on the bed next to him. "Mitchell, put the gun
down. You don't want to do this."

The next words he spat out with fiery rage. "The truth!
Now!"

She tried not to react. She tried not to stare at the metal
in his hand.

He growled, "You're one of them."

Athena held out her hands, trying to be as least
threatening as possible. "I'm not. Not anymore. I promise.
It's not — "

Mitchell's hand tightened on his gun. "Don't say it.
Don't lie to me."

Athena could see the pain in the other's eyes. She knew
that she couldn't lie any more, but she knew the truth could
get her killed.

"It's not real, Mitchell," she said. "None of it was ever
real."

Mitchell shook with rage, but his eyes were pleading.
"You're lying! I have the documents! I have footage! I saw it!
With my own eyes! It's real," then, he added weakly, "It has
to be."

The adrenaline flooding her system, she pleaded, "I'm
sorry, Mitchell. God, I'm so, so sorry."

Mitchell pulled back the hammer on his revolver, and
Athena braced herself for the inevitable.

"It's goddamned real!" he screamed. She closed her eyes. She should hear the rattle of the revolver now shaking in his hand. She could hear the pain in his voice, but she knew it was time. Time for the truth to finally come out.

It was all a lie.

All of it.

Athena shook her head, on the verge of tears. "It's not real, Mitchell. I know."

Her eyes moved from barrel of the pistol and met his eyes.

"I know, because I made it up. All of it," she said. "You pull that trigger, Mitchell, it won't change anything. I can't defend what I did."

"Try," he said. "Is what you said out there true? Your book. Augustus. Did you make it all up?"

She nodded. "I did."

"Liar!"

"Look at the evidence, Mitchell," she said. "The documents, the photos, the Glowaski site. It's all a house of cards. Look closely and it all falls down."

She could see his tick had emerged. Mitchell reached up and touched the scar on his temple as he thought.

"The language," he snapped. "What about the alien language?"

"Done by a designer in Japan," she said. "I can give you his name if you want. It was Seisaku-san."

"The star charts," he said, agitated.

"We hired an astrophysicist and told her it was for a movie," she said, and she saw that Mitchell's grip on his gun relaxed. "Some part of you has to know that I'm telling the truth."

The pistol shifted in his hand. "Why would you do it? Why would you lie to me? Why would you fuck my life? Is there anything that you ever said to me that was true?"

"Yes," she said. "I'm your friend, Mitchell. I wanted this to end, I just didn't know how."

"I do." Mitchell's gun trembled in his hand. "Why? Why goddammit?"

Athena felt ashamed. "Because," she said. "I wasn't given a choice. It was a job, Mitchell. It was just a job."

"It was your job to destroy me?" he asked, weakly.

Athena swallowed. "If you pull that trigger, I'd deserve it. I put you through hell. And I put your family through hell."

"You can't imagine what you did to me," he said. "What your lies did to me. Why? Because it was your job?"

"Because I was ordered to? It was an assignment," she said, then corrected herself. "No, because I could."

"I don't believe you," he said. His hand tightened on the handle of his gun.

"Pulling the trigger won't change the truth," she said.

"You expect me to believe anything you say?" he said as tears flowed down his face. "You've always lied to me. And you're lying again."

"It's the truth," she said. "I swear."

"Swear on what? What do you even believe in?" he challenged. "Anything?"

"I don't know anymore," she said, "but the truth is all I

have left to give you. One last time, Mitchell. Believe me. I'm begging you, believe me. Please, put the gun down."

He was sobbing now, his chest heaving. "My daughter," he said. "She doesn't even know me. This is all I have left. And you tell me it's a lie."

Mitchell raised the gun to his head.

"Mitchell!" she shouted, "Stop!"

"All I have" he whispered, "is a lie."

"Mitchell!" she shouted as he pulled the trigger.

Athena screamed as his head snapped back in a pink mist, and his body slumped to the floor.

— 8.4 —

Police cars, ambulances and fire trucks filled the parking lot of the hotel. The convention attendees were gathered in groups giving the official vehicles a wide berth. Some of them were still in their cosplay. The police had already marked off areas with yellow tape and were milling about assuring them that everything was under control.

Athena watched this from the back of an ambulance with a blanket over her shoulders. The dull pain of tomorrow's hangover creeping in a little early. Someone had handed her a styrofoam cup of terrible coffee. She had held it, untouched past the initial sip, until it grew cold. She had tried to tell the police what happened, but, she had no idea how coherent she had been.

An obsessed fan, she had said. A man who hadn't been well. What she left out, was the fact that she was the one who had driven him to madness.

She saw a man in a black suit approaching from across the parking lot. When the police approached him, he flashed a badge and continued marching towards her. When he got close, he pushed up his fedora, and Athena broke into a smile when she recognized him, which quickly vanished when she realized what his presence meant. He was a little grayer on the temples, and the lines on his face were a little deeper, but Howell was still as handsome as ever.

"What?" she whispered.

"I'm here to get a statement, ma'am," Howell said. He stood at-ease, folding his hands behind his back.

"Smiles," she said. Athena resisted the alternate urges to both hug him and run.

"Good to see you're in one piece," he said.

"What are you doing here?" she asked, pulling her blanket a little tighter around her. "What is this?"

His face darkened. "We need to debrief you after what happened."

"Debrief," Athena repeated. "Does that mean what I think it means?"

"Probably," he said. "You're pretty good at putting the puzzle pieces together."

"Do I have a choice?"

"You've always had a choice," he said. "But, are you

going to make the smart one?" He patted her on the knee and motioned for her to follow.

Athena nodded and set her cold coffee down. "I understand." She shrugged off the blanket and did as he asked. She moved through the parking lot past the flashing lights, and gathered crowds, barely even aware she was doing it. She focused on putting one foot in front of the other. She didn't know what Howell was leading her towards, but, multiple possibilities raced through her mind.

None of them were good.

Howell led her through the busy lobby past the attendees and down the long hallway until they reached the hotel's office center. He came to a closed door with frosted glass, and knocked three times before turning the knob to reveal a small conference room. Athena gasped.

At the far end of the table, Franklin sat deep in thought with his fingers steepled. When she stepped into the room, his eyes flashed and a smile tugged at his lips. He now sported a neat grey beard with a streak of red-blond off-center on his chin. He rose, running his hand down his torso to straighten his suit, and greeted Athena with a tilt of the head.

"Please," Franklin said, gesturing to one one the chairs around the conference table, "have a seat."

Athena felt cold, shaking, as she took a seat as far from Franklin as she could.

As Howell locked the door with a deadbolt, Athena braced herself. "What do you want?"

"I just want to talk," Franklin said. "It's been far too long. And, you've been busy. I read a PDF of your novel off of the publisher's secure server. Exposing yourself to the community with a book that more or less outlines everything you've done. Establishing celebrity within the alien conspiracy elite?"

Athena stared at the man. "Just get this over with," she said. "What do you want?"

Franklin continued without letting her words break his stride. "Your revelation will make them question everything they've ever seen or heard about aliens and UFOs. Now that was either brilliant, or foolhardy. Either way, it certainly got my attention."

"What about Mitchell Vincent?" she snapped. "Was his life worth it?"

Franklin's expression became somber. "An unfortunate consequence in our line of work."

"*Our*," she repeated. "I don't work for you, not anymore. Never again."

"Yeah, about that," he said. "There's still a great deal to be done. New challenges, new stories to tell."

"And if I refuse?" she asked.

Franklin raised an eyebrow and shrugged. "Your sudden disappearance will almost certainly solidify your myth," he said, and Athena couldn't miss the fact that Howell was blocking the door.

Franklin continued, "Now, as to how you disappear, well, that is entirely up to you. Whether you take your place back among the team, or," he gestured to Howell.

"Make the smart choice, Athena," Howell said. Howell put his hands back and pulled his jacket open just enough to make sure his shoulder holster was visible. "Please."

Trapped, Athena stared in horror as a friendly smile spreads across Franklin's face. He spread his arms wide.

"Welcome back to the team."

Made in the USA
Las Vegas, NV
17 February 2021

17909270R10114